RAVEN

AND THE RISING SUN

TESS KIELHAMER

Copyright © 2019 Tess Kielhamer

ISBN:
9781094875323

How can this book serve you Lord?

"Because everyones greatest sins are toward
themselves, and everyones greatest victories are
coming back to who they are."

Introduction

I Would like to dedicate this book to all who have touched the path of my life. To all who feel stripped of their inner light, may you rise and shine brighter than ever before. For only those who have crawled out of the dark nights of their soul and make it to the light can comprehend the truth of the universe.

I would like to thank all of my angels and God for the whispers in my ear.

CONTENTS

CHAPTER 1

THE DESERT FOREVER

Mirages wave through a hot barren desert and over an old deserted western town. Out from the view of a dark window in the town's clock tower Cassidy sees on the horizon several men heading toward the town. She panics as she hastily gets her guns ready and knives prepared in her worn holsters and belt. She prepares herself for this encounter and looks in her hand noticing only one bullet left and looks back out the window breathing heavier now seeing the men heading closer. She heads down the stairs and steps outside standing in front of the tower at the very place her life was torn and her heart left in purgatory. Cassidy looks empty and lost inside yet with a fire behind her eyes that keeps her burdened and empty body moving under her long black jacket.

A man walks up to her stopping nine yards away with some other men behind him. He is dressed in victorian attire with a modern and sophisticated flare. Dark round metal glasses hide his eyes yet still reveal a deceiving and manipulative face. He holds an embellished cane and tips his old black victorian top hat. He is the Magician. Behind him stand five men of curious stature and freakish appearance with a visage of possession. One man less so with his hands tied behind his back. She glares at them through the hard, hot sun seeing if any of them have a soul left as she looks at the shells of people she once knew so long ago.

"Cassidy...," says the Magician. Cassidy pauses momentarily in disbelief he is back after a painfully long time and even hearing her own name spoken is jarring. She whispers back, "What are you here for?" The Magician slowly steps forward replying, "I have a proposal for you dear. But if you don't mind me asking first how has the past couple hundred years or so been here in this lively town? Do you enjoy the immortal life yet?" A subtle laughter escapes his lips with grey serpentine smoke. With fire pouring through her immortal veins she puts her hand on her gun and prepares to shoot. "You evil bastard," she says with her body rigid in suspense. The Magician unaffected by her still looks straight through her eyes and through her soul, "I don't see why you want to waste that last bullet of yours Cassidy." Cassidy looks slightly shocked to realize he knows she has one bullet left. He slowly walks up to her and puts his hand around her gun bringing it toward his heart and brings his face seductively close to hers. He places his other hand gently alongside her face whispering close enough to kiss her, "I would save that last bullet if I were you." Cassidy begins sweating down the side of her face and her heart begins beating like a throbbing thud of a tribal drum. There is so much of her conscience imprisoned that prays to be unshackled but she can only remain this captured bird.

"Now, you never let me get to my proposal," says the Magician still close to her flushed cheek, "I know you must be so tired of being trapped in this town, and I... Well, the thing is

I need more gifted people like yourself to work for me my lady. Like the old days when we were a team. You see as of now you will continue to remain here for eternity, depressed in isolation and praying for death, or… I can make a small break in my spell that allows you to leave here only at night returning upon sunrise if you work under me. Quite cordial of me actually." The Magician smiles to himself and looking pleased with his reasonable offer brushes his gloved hand under her chin.

Cassidy looks relieved for a brief moment with a glimpse of some hope for a life she once had but knowing it is just an illusion of hope she quickly becomes filled with hatred and mistrust as she knows all his true intentions are in a never ending search for more power. Knowing there are many reasons to say no she can't stand being trapped in this ghost town any longer. "What's your catch?" she firmly asks. The Magician grins and steps back to elegantly gesture to the man at his left who is unwillingly present. "To partially break the spell I have on you, you must kill a mortal innocent soul. That's all," the Magician replies with a wide grin.

This victim man immediately shouts, "What the fuck! You can't use me! I work for you! I've been working for you for fifteen years!" screams the panicking man looking around hopelessly for a possible escape. The Magician grabs the man by his neck like easy prey for her to see. The victim man struggles with disbelief and gasping for air. "Shut up," says the Magician in a monotonous tone and void of emotion, "You are just a worthless mortal whose day has come to an end under my command. Your service to me is no longer required." He starts pulling the victim's neck tighter without any effort whatsoever and his short temper makes his grey smoke turn black and slither around the paralyzed man like a bug trapped in a web.

"Well, what will it be Cassidy? Had enough of being here stranded for eternity in your own pity and shame or take your one and only chance to freedom, because I can give you that. It will just take one small sacrifice, only one death. It's quite silly actually." Cassidy starts shaking in a cold sweat and her hand begins quivering with the fateful bullet. "I won't lower myself to you and your corruption," she whispers and points her gun at the Magician knowing he is immortal as well yet still basking in the brief imaginary moment that she would love to end his evil being. Cassidy knows shooting at the Magician would only serve her pain and a blunt ego fixation. "He's immortal," she reminds herself again. She knows the reality is that she has been trapped here for so long and could well be for all eternity. This is truly her only chance but at the cost of her integrity.

Cassidy changes her aim to the victim. Her hand is unbearably shaking now as she aims to the helpless victim's head. Her eyes almost cry and her worn mind is like a loose cannon ready to implode with violence. The Magician in a deep yell rumbling with darkness shouts, "Do it now or forever hold your peace Cassidy! The world will only leave pathetic souls like you to be crushed in the hands of the wicked!" His voice echoes deep into her being and then there is silence as her mind takes her far back into the repressed rabbit holes forgotten in her memory.

FLASHBACK TO
THE BIRTH OF IMMORTALITY

It's a beautiful summer night in the same western town but yet in its prime. The town is alive and sounds of the carnival and circus showcase with laughter. Excitement rings through the desert and people marvel and cheer. Some of the best of times before redemption.

A young handsome man with loving eyes arrives atop the town's clock tower. Cassidy is relieved to see him and they engage in a hug of relief at each others beloved sight for their true love is flawless and complete. Cassidy however senses a different feeling inside like a brick in her stomach for she knows something isn't quite right. "Are you ready to go?" Cassidy asks. "Of course," this young bright eyed handsome man says, "Come here first. Promise me you will stay with me forever." He looks deep into her eyes but something is lingering with an air of deceit. Cassidy looking slightly confused but still so happy and in love replies, "Yes...yes. I promise to be with you forever. I love you." The young man stares fiercely through her, "Then kiss me on that promise. Promise me you are mine for eternity." He grabs her arms tight and pulls her into him. He forces an intense kiss that won't let her pull away and taking her breath. She forces open her eyes and sees her lover transforming into the Magician.

"No...no...," She whispers and backs up away from his arms trembling with eyes wide in disbelief. Cassidy knows of his great powers and she realizes there is a much more sinister plan behind just this kiss as the words, "Promise and forever," cycle through her mind. Cassidy promptly becomes fearful for the man she loves. "Where is he?" she demands. The Magician agitated and impulsive with her question shouts back, "It doesn't matter! Our fate is sealed for eternity dear!" "Where is he? What did you do!" Cassidy screams forcefully in hysteria while tears finally weep down her beautiful, sweet face.

The Magician with his eyes shares and transports with his magic what transpired to her lover for Cassidy to see for herself. Together in suspension they watch her lover performing happily in the circus tent down below as he shows his acrobatic display throughout the air on the ropes swinging from one to another. Fear strikes the young man's eyes as he feels the wicked and heavy air like the smelling of poison. The Magician rests in the wings insidiously as he uses his fingers to twirl the ropes effortlessly about with his conjuring. Instantly through mid air the man is fatefully manipulated and intwined into the acrobatic ropes twisting his neck and hanging him to his death. In mid performance the music ceases and he hangs to his last breath for the whole audience to see. Silence rolls through the crowd as every soul witnesses the horrific death. The Magician then leaves the scene of the terrified crowd and begins transforming into an illusion of the now dead young man.

The Magician then lifts the trance and as she opens her eyes into his he says to her, "Well let's just say he's still on the ropes." "Oh, God no," she says faintly as the audience begins to flee the circus in sounds of fear. She begins shaking to her core and loses her mind in complete hysteria for she can't accept her life without her love and will not be damned to be a slave to the Magician forever. She pauses in her breakdown and with cheeks drenched with tears looks up into the Magician's eyes seeing someone she can not fathom being with or the fate that has befallen her. In a distraught escape she turns to run fearlessly throwing herself off the top of the town's clock tower. Cassidy leaps reaching for peace and falls gracefully with her golden hair dancing through the wind as she closes her eyes to accept ending the pain in her heart she cannot handle or accept.

The Magician jumps down to her broken body effortlessly off the building and lands with ease on his feet without a blink of an eye. Cassidy lays still on her side with her eyes closed. She realizes she hears footsteps in the dirt and feels hollow inside when she knows she unfortunately didn't die and that it is true she is now immortal too. She slowly opens her eyes to see the Magician stepping next to her head as he stands in a puddle of her blood. "You now are eternal like me Cassidy, for it is sealed and cannot be undone. Accept your fate and be by my side my love," he says with his left hand reaching out to her. She lays immobilized with defeat and looks into his eyes again, "I will never love you," she replies and hopelessly tries to get up. Cassidy spits up blood and gravel and lays back down contorted in the dirt, "I will never in my heart have a place for you."

Anger spills over the Magician's face. Feeling utter rejection at his only and last attempt in his life for love. "Cassidy! If you do not agree to be with me, I curse you to be bound to this town forever! I will insure your life to suffering and depressing isolation. So choose wisely," he says rattling from the building fire inside ready to explode into rage and madness. Cassidy looks up at him again, "Never," she faintly replies. "You made a wrong choice Cassidy!" shouts the

Magician and then turns around hiding his face from her. His energy sinks and his mind conspires with his soul. With his back to her he says, "You will truly regret this forever my sweet dove."

Cassidy fearfully crawls away from him and scurries up into the tower. She runs up the stairs to peak out a window overlooking the town. She starts to hear cries and yells from the people and the sound of a murderous rage. Through the small window she can see the Magician's victims being slain everywhere like a battlefield. She feels so helpless and guilt starts to consume her for she feels she is to blame for all of this tyranny. From the top tower window Cassidy can hear the Magician's yells of madness and knows there is nothing she can now do. "You see this Cassidy! This is your choice! Your choice! I am true to my word! Let this lay a burden on your heart and soul forever!" the Magician yells knowing she can hear him from the tower, "You shall remain a caged bird forever!"

Within hours the whole town is slain and it is almost sunrise. She steps outside the building to see the carnage and horror. The Magician is standing out on the far end on the small town with his selected circus servants who decided eternal life under him instead of death. He drops a light of fire on the ground as a circle of flames surrounds the whole entire blood red town instantly with him and his servants standing on the outside of the circle of fire. "This flame shall bind you here forever. Good bye Cassidy," the Magician says to her and his selected few who agreed to be his minions for eternal life turn and walk away into the desert. One of the men who called himself Gunslinger turns around to look her in the eyes with sorrow for he was a like a father to Cassidy. Before he turns back he gives Cassidy a quick nod with the tip of his hat and then disappears with the group into horizon with the hot rising sun.

BACK TO PRESENT MOMENT, DESTINY AND FATE

Her eyes fill with pain of the memories that transpired so long ago and the realization of where she is now and what choices are laid before her. She again looks at the Magician and then the victim man. "Why does he desire me to commit such a hideous sin?" she asked herself. Then she comes to the realization he needs her to have no heart left, void of feelings, and to be yet but a corpse. Like a soulless servant to the Magician. She debates in a timeless moment what both decisions foretell. If she denies this opportunity she will remain in her isolation in the ghost town surely forever and may never receive another chance. If she commits this murder she will partially break the spell that entraps her in this desert and she may leave at night to return by sunrise but only under the Magician's command. Cassidy empties her heart and numbs herself. She only hears silence as the Magician yells her destiny to her in chaos and clamor and then out of the silence she hears the sound of her breath exploding into a loud bang of a gunshot piercing through the forehead of the victim man as he falls to his knees and dies. The gunshot echoes throughout the desert far out of the ghost town and all of the men stand in silence as well. Cassidy stands frozen without a blink of an eye as the high noon sun strikes down onto the gun piercing back into her eye. Her vision blurs and a mirage waves over of the fallen victim man.

The Magician smiles and opens his arms in welcoming, "Well at least you didn't lose your aim Cassidy but it didn't have to be that painstakingly difficult. Get yourself together and show up tomorrow night at the Roosevelt Hotel. You will receive instructions on your task once you arrive from one of my men. Oh yes, don't forget... Only after the sun goes down." Before he turns around again he winks his left eye from the corner of his glasses with his sinister smirk. "Come on everyone let's get out of here, I hate this place. Bad memories here ya know," he says as he signals his crew to get into their vehicles to head out. The last car door slams shut and tails off leaving a cloud of dust lingering around Cassidy as she still stands frozen with her gun still in her hand. No bullets left, just the hot sun and the dust in her face.

CHAPTER 2

ENTRANCE INTO MODERN DAY CITY LIFE

The sun on the horizon lowers between the darkening city setting between two skyscraper buildings like the Stonehenge. The dark orange sun sits heavily outside the window of the Magician's luxurious office overlooking the city as its light reflects through the window onto the nine orange candle flames spread about in the room. The Magician rests in his chair lawlessly planning the next move with his men. The Magician reaches forward to pinch a candle flame putting it out. Smoke rises into the room mellifluously as the Magician controls it with his hand and his mind drifts off to theorize. "Smoke is the life after the flame, is it not? Its departed soul is unfettered by the confinements of the scrupulous," the Magician recites as he eases off into his own world with delusional eyes. He then with a content grin looks up at the men standing before him. "We have a few minor tasks tonight men but I have a good feeling we will be assisted by an old friend of ours, the notorious Cassidy. The quickest knife and blade handler I've known and with eyes like a hawk. Well at least she used to be," he says pausing in thought, "But we shall see. However don't underestimate her. I think I finally broke her annoying will and compassion so hopefully I can finally work with her true potential and expand her magic." He leans forward on his desk crossing his hands looking gravely at the men and speaking sternly, "She has no idea what magic she has potential of. Show her no empathy as she will weaken. Some of you are new here but you original members from long ago know what I'm talking about."

"We really don't need anyone slowing us down," says the Illusionist in his mellow English accent containing his irritation at hearing of Cassidy's return. He has black hair slicked back under his fedora and sharp asian eyes. His suit is pin stripped with suspenders and he has an attractive frame and a quiet face. The Magician instantly becomes irritated at the questioning of his plan. He looks at the Illusionist and slithers smoke out of his right hand moving up around his torso wrapping him up and partially strangling the Illusionist momentarily just for amusement. "Never forget who you work for and who gave you your incredible power. I know what I'm doing and don't question me again," he says leaning back into his chair. He then releases the coiling of smoke letting him gasp for air. "I know you gave me my great power master. So many years ago I was a a child without a home and you found me. My apologies for questioning you master," replies the Illusionist humbly.

The Magician begins shuffling his cards on the desk and looking down says to the men, "Our plan tonight is to expand our dominance through the outskirts of Los Angeles. There are still a few surviving and stubborn gangs that refuse to work under us so they leave us no option. I gave them too many opportunities and they declined. I want you to kill all three of the leading men and you know who they are," says the Magician looking up briefly from the cards to make contact with them, "As well as any others under them who refuse to be of any service to us. All that do not accept our dominion should be destroyed, end of story. That's how we work. I will see you all back here before sunrise," the Magician demands as he stands up to exit the room. "What about Cassidy?" asks an older man appearing concerned. He is in old western attire with a full mustache and greying hair. His face tells a story of wisdom and experience. He is the Gunslinger and often called Slinger. The Magician replies turning his head seemingly unsettled by the question and concern from Slinger, "She will be there, don't worry." He proceeds to inspect the Gunslinger up and down briefly with his eyes as he is unsure of his motive of concern.

The men quickly leave the room grabbing their various weapons and hurry their way getting into a variety of exquisite vehicles. The Fakir steps into and closes the door to an elaborate black 1940's hearse. He is a strong intimidating man dressed in 1920's knickers, vest, and an ivy newsboy cap atop his bald head. He has many exquisite tattoos throughout his body and a handlebar mustache. The Gunslinger gets on a uniquely modified Harley with raised handlebars and several weapon and firearm attachments. He carries on his back one shotgun and two revolvers in a fine gun holster. The Illusionist follows pursuit driving in his, "1955 Bentley R-Type." Waiting until his trusted men drive off on their mission the Magician gets into his beloved Rolls-Royce Phantom and follows behind.

FIRST ENCOUNTER

Loud music passes by from vehicles in the streets of a ghetto and worn down, poverty stricken city. Cars drive slowly by prostitution and drugs infest every corner. A general vibe of lost dreams and empty eyes fulfill the city as it has been spiraling into depravation for many years. The hearse slowly pulls up to park in front of the main club on this street. The Fakir steps out of the hearse and starts to walk in front of the building with his heavy, black, old war boots. Heads turn in silence at his noticeable and hardened appearance as he walks gradually toward the front doors. The Illusionist and the Gunslinger pull up parking behind the hearse and follow in order behind. The Fakir then goes to open the doors and isn't surprised to find they have been locked out. He then kicks open the front door calmly yet with unimaginable strength and stands still in the entry way as the doors collapse.

The entryway is filled with armed gangsters cursing at the Fakir while he composedly lights his cigar and rests it unhurried between his lips. He laughs under his breath with his deep and rusty voice. The Illusionist and Gunslinger start to head around to the back of the building. They split up departing around opposite sides just giving each other a brief nod of understanding the plan. The Gunslinger heads toward the right side of the building and the Illusionist heads around the left.

"Why don't you just leave now... You Freak," says one of the more prominent gang members as he laughs at the Fakir with his friends standing behind him. "All of us combined against just you? Ya weirdo! You freak! Look at you!" He laughs shaking his head and walks away. The Fakir walks forward calmly toward them as the first opponent runs up to him to attack. Fakir easily catches his fist without an ounce of expression on his face and quickly proceeds with an arm break. He then quickly continues forward through the club eliminating anyone in sight. The Fakir enjoys showing off his great skill but it is evident that a wicked nature has taken over him since his work under the Magician. Men begin to continuously smash things against his body but he is the Fakir, pain doesn't exist for him, ever. Yet in fact he easily deflects the pain intended for him back at the same moment of impact. The men begin to realize the harder they try to inflict pain they are crippled within their own attempt and have no choice but to submit, flee, or die.

The Illusionist begins entering a secret back entry door and a body guard stands before him. "I don't think so," says the bodyguard in routine assuming it's just another random guy trying to sneak in. "But look what I have for you," says the Illusionist kindly in his old english accent as he smiles and hands him a handful of pocket change placing it in his hand. "What the fuck is this! I don't want your stupid pocket change weirdo!" the bodyguard yells. Looking thoroughly annoyed at the Illusionist and getting ready to swing his fist his face instantly seizes up. The Illusionist smiles replying, "Who said I gave you pocket change?" The Illusionist laughs in pleasure as he sees the bodyguard look down in horror as the change transformed into hundreds of venomous black spiders. The bodyguard lets out a terrifying high pitch yell and begins to lose control as the hundreds of spiders begin to multiply and cover his entirety. The Illusionist with a unhinged laughter continues to compose himself and then calmly proceeds down into the hallway.

The Gunslinger walks down a trash filled alley along the opposite side of the building and is soon approached and surrounded by five fully armed men and one out of place child trying to join the gang. "Look at this old guy! Looking like a fucking cowboy hero haha! At least we know the Magician's crew is getting weak and old!" says one of the men and they all burst out into laughter. "Well, the ol' standoff never gets old I guess," the Gunslinger says with his rich and rusty, county voice. "Say your prayers old man," replies one of the gangsters as all the men together aim their various array of firearms at him. The Gunslinger quickly grabs both hand guns on his holster and takes down all the men before one mortal man could even blink shooting from his hip. The rapid fire was so unimaginably fast it almost sounded like one gunshot ringing in the air. The one loud mouthed gangster looks up at him from the ground with utter confusion as he spits blood out of his mouth, "But how?" The Gunslinger looking down over him replies, "I've kinda been doing this for a long time. A really long time." The child noticeably only got scrapped by a bullet on the leg, obviously on purpose with precision. The kid lays looking at the Gunslinger as they make eye contact knowing that he sparred his life. The Gunslinger then looks around to make sure his compassion wasn't noticed by the Magician.

The three men the Fakir, Illusionist, and the Gunslinger meet up simultaneously and all continue towards the main office at the back of the club on the top floor. At the same time they all burst through the door to see the Magician already standing there before Miguel the legendary leader of this particular East Los Angeles gang organization. Miguel is covered in tattoos and all throughout his face. He is dressed head to toe in a luxurious tailored suit. His collar is unbuttoned with oil and precipitation on his chest and face. With fear all the prostitutes in the room scurry off and hide as all the Magician's men enter the room.

"So you come here and kill my men, before we can even talk this out? You know that is only a small percentage of my army you freaks!" shouts Miguel with sweat dripping over the Catholic cross tattoo on his forehead. "Well it seems my three men took out your best in under... two minutes," the Magician replies while looking briefly at his pocket watch. "Well I don't give a fuck. I have many more men, and what the fuck do you want anyways!" Miguel yells in a scattered response showing his distress. "What we talked about," the Magician says looking him straight in the eyes. "Ha! So you really think I would just agree to you taking over? Just dominating my area! This my territory man, always has been and always will be. My family has run these streets for too many generations, forget about it," Miguel yells back. He tries to stand up and the Fakir's hand pushes him back into his seat. "What are you waiting for?" The Illusionist demands looking frustrated with the Magician. The Magician tilts his head surprised with the Illusionist who is normally calm in temperament. "I'm waiting... for her," the Magician replies. "You are wasting your time," the Fakir says turning to look at the Magician as well for a response as they are all doubtful. The Gunslinger puts his head down staring at the floor. The Magician turns to see Slinger and notices his newly revealed emotions. He is slightly unsettled by it and takes it mentally into account.

ARRIVAL OF CASSIDY

Footsteps echo loud down the hallway. The Magician knowing it is Cassidy steps back and is pleased to watch the show unfold as he rests his hand on his cane in front of him.

The men turn around to look down the long hallway to see who it could be. Cassidy with a calm yet fierce determination walks toward the room in the same boots from hundreds of years ago hitting the wooden floor hard with each of her subsequent steps. She has blood on her long black jacket, hands, and face. A couple men come running around the corner after her at full speed from behind. She lets them get close enough as she still continues walking forward without a glance to the side. She has an elbow blade attached on her right arm. She dodges the first attack and strikes him in the face with a reverse elbow going through his scull. She grabs the second man and throws him to the ground quickly breaking his arm and then his neck. She continues toward the room saying nothing while looking straight at the gang leader.

Miguel stands up quickly pulling his gun and shouting, "Who the fuck is this bitch and what is she doing here? You adding more freaks to your team?" Miguel is almost drenched in sweat from the dread of his fate as all mortals who live in sin truly fear death. Cassidy still proceeds forward as she grabs a weapon from her left side. She abruptly stops under the entryway door and a small blade is thrown toward Miguel at full speed. The blade is forced to stop hovering and suspended in the air inches away from his forehead and the pervading silence is pain to his ears. Miguel looks at her with nothing to say but acceptance of fate. Cassidy stands with her right hand out manipulating the blade in mid air. She snaps her fingers as the blade is forced into the center of his forehead. Blood trickles down the cross tattoo on his head he falls back into his chair.

The Magician steps forward clapping his hands and piercing the remaining silence. "Very nice my little angel," he says slowly walking to her, "Disappointingly late, but you can make up for that." Cassidy looks at him with a vacant stare replying, "Your magic cant work for everything. Besides, working for you is temporary." She turns to walk away then stops before leaving the room painted with a memory of ungodliness, "I agreed to work for you, but you still will never have my heart."

Cassidy's inner being sinks and her light dims from yet another betrayal of her soul. With depression, guilt, and the knowing that every task she will do for the Magician will keep robbing parts of her in this eternal imprisonment she exits the building in self disappointment. She begins reminiscing of brighter days and with her head lowered she walks down an old street full of bars and ruckus in the wee hours of the remaining night. Eventually swaggering with a bottle in hand she then turns into a bar at the end of the road. Looking totally out of place in her old western attire still horned in fresh blood she walks in heading for the last open stool at the bar. People with good reason begin eyeballing her odd appearance and quickly become still and silent from her foreign presence. She sits down and under her breath says, "Whisky," to bartender as he walks by. She consecutively has drink after drink and the people in the bar decide to just ignore her and rubbing her appearance off as just some looney in a costume. "Don't you think you had enough missy?" says an arrogant man at the bar, "And that ain't your seat by the way." Cassidy sitting with her hat down and looking into her whiskey glass. "I reckon I can do what the fuck I wanna do," she replies and then looks over at him with a detached glare, "I've only waited a couple hundred years to get out of a hell hole to see I'm just stuck in a bigger hell hole than I was before and it's full of assholes like you."

"Wow whats your problem? Ya weirdo," says another one of the men. A third man walks up, "Lets see the pretty face under that hat," the man says as he proceeds to touch her shoulder, "Women don't come in this bar unless they wanna have fun." Irritated at the remarks and the touch she quickly pulls out her holstered knife and thrusts it through his hand pinning it to the table. She swings her other hand blade back toward the other man through his face and thus commencing war in a tavern. Several men immediately begin to attempt to bombard her but she effortlessly annihilates all attempts and is satisfied with her release in the liberating combat. She is ludicrous, senseless, and laughs at all attempts coming her way. She has seemed to have lost it, like an addict in their peak of abuse leaving their conscience behind them. Cassidy leaves the bar in shambles and mayhem behind her and she then exits out the back.

The Gunslinger is waiting out back of the bar for her and disappointed with the girl he knew so long ago. Cassidy sways her way outside and is surprised and to see Slinger waiting. "You better get back before sunrise Cassidy. You know the rule," he says to her. "What time is it?" she asks as she wipes blood from her mouth and stumbles around. "It's an hour and thirty minutes till sunrise. Also the Magician wants to meet you tomorrow night at this address." He hands her a small piece of paper. She goes to grab it from his hand and without letting it go he looks her straight in her eyes with genuine care, "It's good to see you again Cassidy. You know... you don't have to act like that." She looks back up at him still holding the paper with him, "You don't know what it's like," she replies. "Yes I do. You forget I am under the same spell Cassidy," he says. She looks back down, "You weren't trapped and isolated in that town for hundreds of years just watching the carnage slowly rot that the Magician left behind. Nobody to talk to. Nothing. Just everything died but I was left in purgatory." Slinger replies softly, "You're right Cassidy I wasn't, and I can't begin to imagine what it was like. But you are here now, back in this world. Please don't lose your soul." She snatches the paper fully from his hands, "I'm afraid it might already be gone." She walks down the alley and stumbles around the corner as the Gunslinger watches in pain. She then walks out of the city down an empty road back to her home. The sun is almost peaking over the horizon with a deep purple sky as she slowly dissipates in the distance of this lonely road like a desert's mirage as dawn comes to light.

DAYLIGHT AT HOME, MEMOIRS OF A PHOTOGRAPH

Daylight seeps through the cracks of her old bedroom window creating a dusty golden mist in the room. She walks up to her window and lets the sun warm her face. Relaxing for a moment a large raven flies close to the window passing it and lands at the building across from her. The raven seems to be observing her as they have a brief juncture and introspection. She shakes her head at the oddity and proceeds to take off her bloody, black jacket and boots while walking to her sleeping corner to fall down on the bed in relief. She then reaches under her bed to grab a photo that sometimes brings her mild comfort. The aged photograph shows herself and her old friends she performed with and some that are still with the Magician now. "All seemed joyous and lively back then," Cassidy reminisces to herself. She notices the smile on her face in the photo and the memory of everyones happiness is bittersweet to her now. It brings an ardent longing for the past to her as she zooms in on the photo and slips into a flashback to the day of the photograph.

FLASHBACK

It is early in the day and everyone is busy practicing something for the evening show. Sounds of joy and laughter are pleasantly throughout the camp. People are busy and focused on their art and performance at hand. Cassidy is busy throwing her knives into a dart wall with perfection. "You're good, but not great yet," says a much older man smiling at her. He is a noble man with legendary martial arts knowledge who has taken Cassidy under his wing. Cassidy turns around with a smirk, "Well you're great, but you're no good!" Kong chuckles, "Ok Cassidy let's go over our routine now. One last time."

They start rehearsing a choreographed fight with various weapons that showcases their extreme and unusual skill in weapons, martial arts, and acrobatics. He is hard on her and expects much. Kong then stops near the end of the routine and heads over to her. "Cassidy...There is a reason in life some of us are great martial artists, and it's not just for circus shows," he says to her. Cassidy appearing surprised at his grave change in tone responds, "What are you talking about? I love doing these shows here with all of you. I am having the time of my life!"

Kong looking concerned at her continues, "I mean you are different. Your fate is written in the star traveling east to west and dark to light. You will know what I mean someday. I have been teaching you since you could walk and I won't be around forever Cassidy. I used to be frustrated being treated like a performance monkey here. When you came into my life I realized what my purpose truly was." Cassidy is bothered by the thought of him leaving someday and understands he is getting very old. "Stop it. I don't wanna talk about this nonsense," she hastily replies. He speaks now even more quietly and in gravity, "There is someone whose darkness will reveal itself soon and last until true light can birth from the utter depths to conquer and subdue its dark plan." Cassidy looks at him straight and more concerned now as he looks back at her earnestly. She knows Kong is an intuitive teacher and that he has her best interest at heart. She absorbs and holds onto the message.

"Alright! Everybody get on in and over here for this new fancy photograph machine!" yells the Gunslinger calling out to everyone rehearsing. Everyone gets into the photograph holding each other with joy as the photographer steadies his equipment and ducks under the black fabric behind the machine. The flash goes off and pulls Cassidy out of her flashback. She wakes up on her bed and looks at the photograph one last time before she goes to place it back under her bed. Right before she sets it away she notices a small raven atop the building in the background right on top of the town's clock tower. She is perplexed and thinks it's quite odd that she never noticed this raven before, nor that the clock was at three in the afternoon in the photograph. Cassidy looks back out the window to see the sun setting and puts her jacket back on and loads her guns and other various weapons. She reads the note the Gunslinger gave to her, "For tomorrow nights mission meet me at the Golden Bay Casino."

CHAPTER 3

ANOTHER MISSION,
BETRAYAL OF SELF

Atop of a golden embellished casino rests the Magician like a king in a throne. He peers out the window watching the sun set behind the city buildings and then looks back at the clock behind him on the wall while he leisurely puffs on his big cigar. He feels accomplished and satisfied gaining control over such a city and even more so finally Cassidy under his thumb. The sun disappears behind the horizon and the remaining light fades away. He watches the clock patiently as thirty minutes pass sunset and he knows she will arrive any second. He puts out his cigar and as the smoke permeates the room Cassidy appears at the door entry. He seems pleasant and relieved to see her however for Cassidy, her blank and absent emotions show otherwise.

"Where is everyone?" asks Cassidy. The Magician raises his eyebrows, "A hello and a thank you would be respectful my lady. To answer your inquiry they are already sent out on their tasks for this evening," he says as he turns to look back out the large window," You see, very soon I will own all of Los Angeles, and thats just the beginning. I am already implementing the next steps to seize governments and so much more from there. Not that it was ever difficult for me, it's just that now is the time. It's lengthy to explain but my increasing and subsequent victories wont stop," he says turning to face her again with a hushed grin. "So what am I doing?" Cassidy replies. "Well first I just wanted to talk to you beforehand. I was so very impressed with you last night. Especially when I followed you on your extra party smashing at the bar. It made the headlines before I did," he laughs and throws down a newspaper in front of her. Cassidy looks at the newspaper headlines in bold and her core drops in remorse of her consequential actions as she reads, "Local Terrorist. Woman dressed in black country attire viciously kills dozens at local bar."

As she begins reading the article and observing the photos revealed from that night the Magician walks around behind her and breathes on her neck. He places his hands on both of her shoulders pulling her back into him. "I missed you so much Cassidy," says the Magician. Cassidy becomes instantly repulsed and slams the paper back down on the desk, "Well keep missin' me because whoever Cassidy was died a long time ago thanks to you." She then turns around to face him, "I have no love to give you. It died in my unbearable isolation, and even if I did..." The Magician with heavy eyes and a breath away from her lips seeps smoke out from his mouth as it wraps around her neck squeezing her and holding her briefly hostage and breathless. "Shhhhhh... Don't ruin this moment Cassidy," he says to her. His smoke coiling around her manipulates her bluntly into his arms as he licentiously tries to kiss her unopened mouth. The Magician becomes frustrated with her stubbornness and forces her against the wall. He progresses to grab her body like a hungry carnivore as she struggles to break free from the chains of his magic. His tongue aggressively makes way into her mouth and over her neck. Admitting her refusal to himself the Magician then steps back. The smoke dissipates as Cassidy finally gasps for air catching her breath.

"One day you will see that you are meant for me. To be by my side. Your powers with my powers together. You won't have to be alone anymore Cassidy." Cassidy breathing heavily with her head down replies, "Who said I was alone? I am content now living accompanied by my own insanity." She then starts furiously grabbing her weapons of choice from his room in a rush to get this night over with in hopes for a glimpse of more freedom. "Make sure you find the owner of this casino for me. Kill him and whomever is in your way. That is your task for me this evening and then find me when you are done. If you execute your mission I might grant you more freedom," he says grinning at her, "And Cassidy, if you can really put on a show for me I promise to give you more liberties out of your cage. Just put your heart to the side. Hush it to sleep like a baby and you will be free from the pain and guilt. Trust me," the Magician assures to her. Cassidy thinks about the freedoms she could have and possibly her old life again. She storms out of the room anxious to get this all over with. "Hopefully this will be the last mission I have do for him," she says to herself in an effort to partially lift the guilt of this premeditated event.

She walks toward the elevator with warm adrenaline building. As the large metal door finally opens she looks up to see Slinger leaning against the wall inside the back of the elevator. "What are you doing!" she whispers to Slinger in irritation as she steps inside. "Cassidy you don't have to do this," Slinger says to her. She can barely bring herself to look back at him to reply, "It's already done. I'm different now." Slinger holding back his frustration replies, "No your not! You have a good soul! I've known you since you were a little girl. You... You are the only one that has an opportunity to make a change out of this. Remember Kong? What would he want you to do Cassidy?" Slinger asks. Hearing Kong's name twists her insides and her eyes welt up, "Well I'm sure Kong had no idea of the things that would happen to me. You know one soul can only take so much until they break. Do you know what you're risking right now anyways? Do you know what he would do to you if he heard you talking like this?" she says now turning to him with grave concern in her eyes, "He would torture you. Eternally!" Slingers voice starts to escalate as he can't handle to see her integrity dwindle away like this, "You're better than him, stronger than him, and smarter than him. He is afraid of your powers Cassidy! Don't fall for the promises of the wicked. I for one don't remember a Cassidy who was ever afraid of someone!" Cassidy gets out of the elevator and looks back over her shoulder as the Gunslinger hides back behind the closing door.

Cassidy proceeds forward stepping out of the elevator. Immediately three large bodyguards begin intensely sprinting toward her like knights running into battle. Someone in the casino yells in panic aloud, "That's her! That's her! Everyone run!" Cassidy's eyes swiftly glance to the side to see who and why someone would say this. She sees eyes everywhere horrified of her presence. Deeply hidden inside her innermost being she still feels she is a good person. The noble loved soul she was once was. "Why the terror in their eyes at me? I'm one of the good guys!" she thinks to herself. This afflicts her deeply as if twisting the spear in her side.

Quickly snapping out of her internal struggle just in time the first bodyguard rapidly goes to reach for his pistol. Cassidy without a flutter of her eye fires low from her revolver at her hip. With perfect aim she shoots before he even gets a chance to pull and fire his gun. She sees the seemingly innocent man drop and reassures herself, "This is the last time. I will be free soon." Instantly from the sound of the first gunshot all guards and agents swarm into subdue her. Cassidy continues forward with ease as her blades and firearms incinerate all on her path with eyes void of her light.

Cassidy appears as if she is in a trance and continues viciously through the casino attacking anyone coming at her with unimaginable and unstoppable skill. Throughout the red carpet of bloodshed on her direct path her mind keeps reflecting to the abominable onslaught on the fateful night the Magician desecrated the village and put her through hell. The built up emotions pours through her as liquid flames as she burns her way through the crowd. People scream and run from the monster she became and her motions become robotic as she sets aside her heart to be freed from the conflict and torment.

She finally bombards her way to the back of the casino and sees the last door ahead of her. She bursts through the final door and her entry collapses all chatter in the room. Her savage presence is unnoticeable to her as she is a fraction of the woman she was yet all pause at the barbarous soul standing before them. Anxious to finally complete her task she is surprised to see the Magician sitting next to the casino owner who remains motionless in his chair with a red blindfold over his eyes. He has a cigar resting in his open and unmoving mouth. The rest of the men remain still and quietly observe her. She contemplates their muted observation of her and immediately becomes troubled thus stirring her deepest afflictions. She wonders if it is that maybe they feel badly and compassion for her like how her old friends would have or is it just her own self shock and mental collapse that is just amusing to the ones she used to call friends.

Cassidy slowly lets her eyes transcend up out of the trance as she realizes more clearly exactly where she is now and all begins to focus again. "You disgust me Cassidy," says the Magician as he leans forward, "You look like an old mangled alley dog. There is nothing beautiful or desirable about you dear. Your an embarrassment to my team. At this moment I don't know why I resurrected you. Clean up your act, your image, and your method of assassination. It's sloppy, you look sloppy, and it's not my standard." Cassidy's eyes spin inside her from his scourging words. She wonders why he made promises to her just moments prior and she then promptly remembers the words from Slinger, "Don't fall for the promises of the wicked." She already felt raw inside from violating her will becoming the beastly savage she just witnessed and hadn't processed it yet and now the slashing regret of trusting the darkness's words of promises. Expecting praise she just becomes torn down and beaten even more, feeling like all she had just sacrificed of herself was for nothing. "Why did I fall for the reaching of hope yet again?" Cassidy contemplates. She then slants her eyes down contemplating her attire and what he said to her and grasping the notion she indeed doesn't look favorable at all. The grand warrior she is becomes crumbled in spirit for she has fallen.

The Magician sits back into his chair, "I said to find this man right here," he says angrily pointing his finger at the man, "You took too long." Cassidy utterly confused replies looking at a clock on the wall, "But how? I just left your room six minutes ago. I had to kill all that was in my way like you wanted and asked for. You said, 'If I really put on a show...'" The Magician ignores her words and cuts her off as he continues speaking, "The Illusionist will be taking over this casino anyways and Mr. Grey here has agreed to sign over everything to me. Oh, and he's already dead. He seemed to suffocate on some smoke this morning somehow, who cares. Anyways now that I finally have everyone here we need to discuss our progress thus far. We have the Fakir now running the east from the, 'Central Street Club.' The Illusionist will be running this west side of town and this casino as his headquarters. I am positioned in the south. You Cassidy will have a big job in the north this weekend."

"Wait... Why did you have me do all of that if you already killed him anyways? For what?" yells Cassidy. The Magician puffs out some smoke as he carelessly replies, "For my amusement. In fact I had all the guards and agents warned about your arrival as well. I even showed them the newspaper of you. That a savage would enter the casino and that she should be stopped! That she is a dangerous criminal! Ah, haha! You see Cassidy I want and need the public to fear and hate you because you are actually good inside and I don't like that. If I am to not built your image to all as a monster, well I know you and I don't need a hero in this town." Cassidy consumed with disgust and bitterness replies, "Well don't expect to be amused again! I'm not your fucking entertainment!" she shouts. "Don't tell me you think you're in control of your life, your path, and your soul because you're not," says the Magician, "I need to wear you down as much as I can until I know nothing left of the old you remains whatsoever. Should you know Cassidy, I was the one who took photographs of you at the bar. I sent them to the media."

Cassidy unrestrained dives forward full speed to fight him out of pure indignation. The Illusionist promptly steps in front of her right before her fist strikes the Magician blocking it. She quickly counters his block and pins the Illusionist's head on the table. She stares back at everyone at the table to see the Illusionist still sitting peacefully in his chair smiling at her. The room pulsates in her cracking mind as she then looks at her hand where his head was. A pumpkin lays under her hand in mockery. Making her feel even more so humiliated the Magician calmly says to her, "It's time for you to go home Cassidy. Start making yourself look a little better while you're at it." He looks her up and down with disgust, "Should you know, if you ever try to take me down you will have to get through all of my people first. However moving forward I will send forth a notice of your next mission and you have no choice but to obey," he says, "The sun will be rising shortly. It's time for you to go."

CHANGE AT HOME

Cassidy arrives home thoroughly exhausted mentally and physically and morning light from the east begins to trickle through the windows painting her room golden. She quenches her thirst with fresh water as she accepts what transpired in the night. Hours pass in mental catharsis while she lays on her white linen bed with wide eyes processing the Magician's words and motives. With every passing subsequent thought she questions her purpose, pains, and fears. She hears a creak in the old dusty wooden floor and turns to see Slinger standing in the doorway. "I rushed as fast as I could to get here. I need to make sure you are alright. Cassidy, I'm afraid for you. I feel like you are falling too deep into the Magician's demoralizing traps and I don't want it to be too late," Slinger says to her with a troubled face as he places a note with an address on her dresser. Cassidy replies laying on her side, "Please don't care. Just go away." Slinger steps forward, "No. I won't. I watched you grow up, and I'm not gonna watch you grow into a monster like the rest!" As Slinger says the word, "Monster," it drops her heart to the bottom of the earth and she replies, "I don't have many options if you haven't noticed." "Oh Cassidy," says Slinger, "Some will see a blooming flower and think only of its death and some will see its one thousand seeds."

The Gunslinger gazes into her eyes finding that child he knew and says, "When you were first hiding in this tower trembling from the death of your mortality and we were all in the battle below awaiting the ring of fire. The Magician gave everyone the option of joining him for eternity or death as you know. However Kong came over to me in the chaos. Before he chose death he gave me orders to stay and watch over you. He said to me, 'Your fate in life was vital. That you were to be a protector watching in the night and a hero to many under the sun. A new source of light.' He said that to me in secrecy right before the Magician killed him. I will be watching you Cassidy. I promised Kong. I didn't know what he meant then but I think I do now." Slinger can see Cassidy's eyes beginning to grow back with a bit of light inside again. He grins at her before leaving and says, "I hope someday you will realize how great you are."

She listens to him head down the stairs as she heads over to open her bedroom window releasing a gentle breeze inside her home. She watches him leave with discomfort and hope paralleled within her secret self. Veering off to view her beloved sun she then witnesses yet again a large raven across the way on the opposite building observing her through the window.

Cassidy reads the note Slinger placed on the dresser reading, "The Magician's mansion 777 Roebuck Lane." She then goes to take off her clothes laying them on the bed and observing indeed how very old and worn they are, not to mention hideously stained with blood and dirt. She heads over to her antique dressers to search for new attire but only finds old fashioned western dresses and such from hundreds of years ago or her old cowboy getup and realizes with either of her options she would appear to be in costume to most people. Cassidy then heads over to the full length mirror to look at her almost naked body admiring her permanent state of youth and prime. It hasn't changed one bit since her day of immortality. She steps forward looking a bit closer into the mirror and is bewildered to see that she is actually becoming more lucent and beautiful. She notices that her eyes seem a bit more golden than before and she then scans her body looking for old scars and yet cannot find one. She breathes in as she pulls back her hair and is slightly startled to see her hair has become much lighter than before as well. Very confused with the emerging and subtle transformation she shrugs it off as so many things are overwhelming to her in her new world and her new life.

Watching the sun finally go down toward the west and waiting to be released from her cage Cassidy anxiously watches every second of the light fading behind the horizon. She then promptly leaves heading east to west toward the inner city along the dusty country road hidden to mortal men. Roaming the city streets in her same shattered, black, and crusty with blood country attire Cassidy searches for clothing stores throughout the night. She wanders about the streets completely mindless to all the frightened onlookers as she gazes into all the boutique clothing stores. As she peers into the windows of the stores that seem so foreign and odd to her many of the store owners close their door as she passes by. With disappointment she moves from one store to the next.

At the bottom storefront window of one particularly upscale store she sees a poster with her image pictured from her recent event at the casino. On the poster it reads, "Dead or Alive $432,000." She swallows her heart into her stomach and drops her head. She knows of course this is the Magician's doing. Him purposely tarnishing her image like he confessed. She wonders in deep concern, "He doesn't do anything at all without a deeply layered plan and at least four steps ahead." She then continues forward to the very end of the street and there is just one shop left to see. She slowly walks in with an assumption she will get thrown out but, "It's worth a shot," she thinks. She immediately notices a long black seductive gown garnished with gold and diamonds and with a sculpted bodice for a ballerina. "It's gorgeous," she thinks to herself as she walk over in awe and glides her hand down the dress. She has never in her life felt a fabric so soft to the touch.

"That is a very special dress dear," says an old, crackly, woman's voice across the room. Cassidy turns to see a gypsy looking woman in her seventies with scarfs of many colors decorating her head. "What are you looking for sweetheart?"

asks the old woman. Cassidy is paused in silence as nobody has talked sweetly to her in so long. "Well?" the woman asks again. "I...I guess I need to clean up and look better ya know. Like everyone else," replies Cassidy. "Why do you want to look like everyone else when you are so very different than everyone else? My name is Anna, and yours is?" Anna asks. "My name is Cassidy," she replies. "Ok Cassidy, try on some of these with this over her and let's start from there," says Anna as she hands Cassidy an armful of different pants and tops. Cassidy grabs everything and heads into the fitting room. After several different options they review in laughter Cassidy becomes lifted by the normalizing feeling of just simply laughing with somebody. Finally after an hour of options Cassidy steps out of the fitting room with streamline black fitted pants showing her defined strong legs and a small, seductive, black vest revealing her sexy yet supernatural fighters body. Cassidy's light hair cascades over her shoulders and lower back contrasting the dark with the light. Anna is taken back at how stunning Cassidy is. "This is it!" says Anna, "I hope you can afford it," she says with a wink.

Cassidy still straps back on her holsters with her blades and pistols over the new clothing. She slides back on her old black country boots because no one will dare take those from her. Cassidy walks up to the counter to pay and before asking the price she hands Anna seven solid gold coins of old. Anna is pleased looking down on the counter at the pure gold before her as she graciously accepts. "Let me clean these old clothes for you too dear. Come get them when you will," Anna says to her kindly. Cassidy hands her all the old bloody clothes and her beloved jacket. "You can trust me," says Anna happily and content with the gold she received from Cassidy. "You know

Cassidy, I think you would look absolutely stunning in the dress you were looking at when you first walked in. I think you should have it actually. It couldn't look better on anyone else. I think it was made for you." Anna smiles and then bags up the dress for Cassidy. "See you soon Cassidy," says Anna. "Indeed!" Cassidy happily replies. She turns to leave and on her way out her eye catches a flyer posted in the window for a late night poetry bar and cafe. She reads the address on the flyer, "936 South Street." Cassidy smiles internally and she feels a zephyr of optimism through her as she makes a mental commitment to visit this enticing place.

CHAPTER 4

MAGICIAN AT HIS LAIR.
PITY FOR THE PUPPETEER

The Magician is resting in his overly lavish and prodigal mansion. His twelve most trusted servants are scattered about in a large room decorated gold with the finest detailing. Towering columns reach the high ceiling painted with divine tribulation and all four walls have extraordinary doors to each of their element. He seats himself in his ancient throne adorned with red velvet seating and standing before him are the flesh to quench his satiety and power. The petrified prey at his feet are two wealthy and renowned men who are owners of a very prominent bank. "Please we will give you anything you want," they beg in desperation to the Magician. The Magician appears unamused and slouches deeply into his chair as he signals with a quick gesture of his hand to the Puppeteer whom is sitting off to the very far side of the room. "It's entertaining watching mortal men who worshiped the material come to such an epiphany and beg for what was always free," the Magician says to the men. "Men wait until their heart is in remorse to grasp the waters that already passed them by."

The Puppeteer across the room fancies a plaid matching suit with a bow tie and a carnation in his suit's front pocket. He is unusually long limbed and has a childish face. It is obvious to anyone the Puppeteer is not mentally stable. He rocks back and fourth on the side of the room mumbling to himself in incoherent verbiage. Self confidence has never been present in this man and thus a perfect vessel for the Magician. The Magician signals again this time pointing to the two bank owners. The Magician then finally responds to the bank owners, "You should have handed everything over to me the first two times we asked you. Three times is too late, and three you see is the magic number. So now, suffer till' death. Thats what I want." The Magician smiles wide leaning forward and resting his chin into his hand preparing for his kind of show. The Puppeteer starts his tale with his puppet strings and giggling away to himself in the corner. The two men start swinging violently at each out of their will as puppets in this show and tears drench the grown men's faces. As the performance progresses the Puppeteer spirals deep into his psychotic smile which signals to those who know him it is far too late for anyone at this point under his spell. The Magician throws a small razor blade on the floor at their feet as he walks up holding a pen and paper contracts. "Time to sign everything over to me. On your own free will that is!" says the Magician bursting into laughter.

CASSIDY'S THIRD ARRIVAL

Cassidy arrives for her first time to this prodigal mansion of his. Her heart beats louder than her thoughts as she walks up to the large towering front doors guarded by two masked men. One mask silver in sorrow and despair and the other of gold in laughter and joy. She enters carefully as they graciously open the heavy black doors for her and she quietly proceeds inside. Searching the halls for the Magician throughout the mansion she hears the Magician's shilling laughter echoing off the walls and follows pursuit. Finally arriving to the Magician's ballroom she peers through a crack in the doors and with distress she begins to observe the torture and humiliation. Her face cringes and her insides twist as she can barely handle watching and hearing the torment that he enjoys so dearly. Her heart tells her to go inside and do all she can do to stand up for these innocent people, but she feels that she cannot. With her heart saying yes and fear screaming no Cassidy is painfully muted in any action. The inner foundation of her spirit has been broken down too much and she feels powerless. With a crushed will she can only watch in shame.

The first bank owner whimpers as he is forced like a doll to pick up the razor and heads over to the other man grabbing him by his arm. With the small blade he begins engraving in his arm the name, "The Magician," and proceeds to do the same carving on his own arm well. Without an ounce of spirit left in them from the physical and mental torture they proceed to sign the documents unwillingly by the Puppeteer's manipulation which hand over the bank in its entirety to the Magician. "Thank you," says the Magician as he ever so slightly bows as if he made a formal business deal. He then signals again a quick gesture to the Puppeteer. The Puppeteer understanding the gesture begins a hideous and insecure laughter revealing his fragile mental state. "I am not that bad, I am not bad. I'm really not that bad!" yells the Puppeteer to himself over and over again in different enunciations searching for mental comfort. He then twirls his hands and pulls the strings as he twists their necks effortlessly breaking them one at a time as they fall to the floor.

The Puppeteer completing the Magician's direct order then sits down on the floor with wide and dilated eyes. He holds himself rocking back and fourth quickly as he laughs with his head down obviously flooded with guilt and confusion like an abused child breaking in every direction in his mind. The Magician walks over to the Puppeteer towering over him and whispers, "Look at you. You're pathetic. You have the potential to be quite exceptional, maybe one of my favorites, but like this you will always be nothing." The Puppeteer then buries his head deep into his knees sobbing.

The room lay quite yet filled with many. Many not knowing who is silent in disgust with the Magician or muted out of fear of him. The Magician then breaths out heavy lifting the Puppeteer into the air with a stream of smoke. Some hide their expressions from the Magician and cringe at knowing he abuses this puzzled soul routinely because he can and yet there is no righteous soul to stand up. Cassidy however can no longer handle this wrongdoing and stand aside. Her innermost feeling of lack of power transmutes to dignified anger. She forcefully enters the room and the large heavy doors slam behind her causing all heads to turn. She stands confidently in the room with sharp eyes penetrating forward intently at the Magician. "Are you done torturing the Puppeteer?" she asks in a demanding tone. The whole room including the Magician are struck with her presence as her courage ripples through the silent air and all take notice of her alluring transformation.

"Cassidy," says the Magician with a pleasant smile. He bows his head forward lifting off his hat, "You look so beautiful," he says from across the large room. He places his hat back on and continues, "Shame on you though for breaking our covenant and interrupting me. You should know better dear." Filled with resentment of her courage he then back fists his left hand through the air. His magic effortlessly throws her across the room like a rag doll slamming her back into the marble wall. Cassidy slides down the now cracked marble wall and hits the hard cold floor. She is momentarily breathless but surprisingly attempts to gather herself gradually. "You know me too well Cassidy," he says nonchalantly as he strolls over to her across the huge room. His elaborate shoes echo with each step through the breathless room as he slowly takes off his white gloves. "As you know Cassidy, the night only lasts so long and you still have a very important task tonight under my command. A task that could put you leading my crew, my army, and my empire for me by my side. That is if you succeed, and it's probably a good idea to start behaving dear. You are so very stubborn and don't realize you would find peace in complete succumbing to me."

Still laying against the wall Cassidy coughs up blood and opens her eyes just enough to look at him. "Don't give me that look Cassidy," he says, "I made you immortal. I can do what I want and please with you. You will be just fine." Cassidy starts to stand up and looks back at the damaged wall. She then notices all eyes in the room are on her in anticipation. Inside she is quite surprised of her withstanding the intensity of the slam. She looks back at him and says, "And what is it exactly that you want me to do now?" The Magician steps closer to her and with desirous eyes he reaches out to run his hand softly over the side of her cheek he hit. "Here is a photograph and an address," he says placing it into her hand, "He is the one last man who is pulling some stings in this town that are in my way. I need him eliminated and you're perfect for the job. I already dominated most of what I need but to complete my rulership thus far there is just that one last man standing in my way. His name is Mr. White. I gave him a chance to easily sell out but he prefers death I suppose." "Why can't you do it?" asks Cassidy. The Magician replies, "I am the master manipulating both sides of the chess board. My hands in battle are unnecessary." "So are you admitting to me your manipulation?" she asks. "No, because I've never given you a choice Cassidy. You're already in my game. It's a paradox," he says with his face so close to her now his lips reach yet an inch away from hers, "I am sure you will perform wonderfully tonight my dear one."

Cassidy begins breathing heaver filling with vexation of spirit. Leaning into his ear and with her cheek laid upon his her warm breath says into his ear firmly, "No," she whispers. The, "No" permeates and bleeds throughout the room shattering expectations. He is silently enraged by her remaining stubbornness and growls deeply within as he coils smoke from his left hand. The smoke begins to cocoon her from the ground up. He dives into his licentious pleasure of punishment as it slithers around her neck and starts to compress her like a snake. She gasps for air while squealing like an animal and blood trickles from her nose and mouth. The Magician then releases the coiling smoke and she collapses yet again. The whole room still lay silent in observation for no one has ever said, "No," to the Magician. The original members watch apprehensively as they know of his wanting and desire of her and the complexity of the situation. Yet all lacking courage they remain still and muted.

"Take this as a warning sign to all of you who are eager to feel independent from my wrath," says the Magician as he looks briefly around the room, "I'll forget you said that Cassidy because time is of the essence tonight. Now if you do complete your task with perfection you shall be rewarded greatly." "How do I know you won't just humiliate me like you did in the Casino? That was all futile and vain," replies Cassidy. The Magician now putting back on his glove responds to her, "It was not unnecessary Cassidy. I had to make sure you were willing to do as I had asked. I had to humiliate you in the meantime as well to keep you in check of where you stand with us. Keep your eye on the prize Cassidy and remember to quiet your heart."

MR. WHITE,
A MORTAL MAN

Cassidy leaves the room and wipes the blood off her face. As soon as the doors she entered through slam behind her she looks at the photograph of the man and the address that was given to her reading, "1116 Annwn Road." She charges out of the building and sees several vehicles belonging to the Magician parked out front. She finds a black motorcycle that suits her for now and with the keys still inside she blasts off to her destination. Slinger watches from around the corner with a careful eye waiting for her to leave. After being sure there are no eyes around to notice he quickly jumps on his bike to follow her pursuit.

She arrives at a gorgeous mansion with few lights still remaining on from inside. The elegance of the surroundings stupefies her momentarily and she reads the address on the magnificent gates before her. She gracefully unheard and unseen passes the tall gate and waits amongst the greenery behind the mansion in a beautiful garden debating her best entry. The sheltered and loving visage of the scenery makes her mind wander to fond dreams of a family. Something her soul has never touched. The aura is so comfortable and peaceful she breathes in the moment and closes her eyes from her own reality. She hears children's laughter coming from inside and decides it would be best go through a particular window she notices in effort to hopefully avoid the children.

Cassidy waits out back perched under a tree until the remaining house lights begin to go out. After making it threw the small window she weightlessly glides through the halls as light as a feather to find the master bedroom. Just in time she slips into the master bedroom and waits patiently in the shadows behind the closet door. The man walks into his room, closes the door, and begins to undress dropping his suit on the floor. He heads into his bathroom with a sigh and starts his shower. He takes a long shower letting warm steam fill and calm the atmosphere. Twelve minutes pass and he finally steps out of the shower, puts on his robe, and then heads back into the room to sit at a desk by his bed. He proceeds to open a book with an exterior of white leather and begins to read where he left off previously.

Cassidy still unseen speaks out of the shadow, "Please don't make any noise." Fear afflicts the man's eyes. "Are you one of the Magician's thugs?" he asks in dread. "I don't consider myself that," replies Cassidy. "Well you are all monsters! Freaks! The Devil's work..." replies the disheartened man. Cassidy steps forward out of the shadow and into the light. The man is stunned to see her beauty as he was expecting differently. "No... I'm a great gal. I promise I will make this quick so I can go back to my monster's cave," Cassidy says sarcastically. The man looking more into what hides behind her face asks her, "Why do you work for that devil?" He closes his book and sets it on the desk. "It's...complicated," replies Cassidy while noticing the emblem of an owl on the cover of his book. Reluctant to explain herself she knows he wouldn't even begin to grasp her journey to why and who she is now. "Everything can be complicated if you look at it complicated. But it's actually very simple. It's a choice. We all have choices and freewill. The only person who holds us from ourselves is ourselves... So when exactly did you make the choice to be a coward?" asks the man. Cassidy implodes running up to him yelling in defense to her fragile shell, "How dare you! You know nothing of me! I am... I am... I... I am stronger than you could ever imagine!" The man yells back at her, "Well if your so strong then do it already! Get it over with!"

Bursting into the room is a little boy and little girl appearing five and seven years old alarmed from the noise. They stand in the doorway paralyzed to see this woman standing over their father. "Daddy! Daddy I need you daddy!" shouts one of the children. "Don't hurt our daddy!" screams the other, "You're just like the bad guys that took our Mommy away!" Tears overwhelmingly fill his light blue eyes. "Go to your rooms now! Daddy is going to be okay. Now I said!" he yells at his children. The children scurry off to their rooms crying and slam their doors. He turns back to face Cassidy, "So why are you waiting?" he says in mourning. Cassidy is shocked and her eyes tremble. "What happened to their mother?" she asks. "Your friends or whoever you work for killed her as a threat to me. If I didn't vow to give up my position in power... Well, the thing is they never even really gave me a chance to... The next day I got a picture of her dead. Not just dead but suffocated to death with no marks. This was just three years ago. I'm surprised you don't know about it. Why?" he then asks reluctantly as he drops his head hiding his remorse. "Like I said," replies Cassidy, "It's complicated. I guess all I can say is I wasn't really around for a very long time."

"Well whatever it was, just promise me one thing. Make sure they are okay. They are innocent beautiful children. Their hearts are only full of love and innocence. Something that you, well you just don't have," he says to her. Cassidy moves her way to stand behind him and slowly pulls out her blade up to his neck. She breaths heavily as pain like no other shoots through her damp heart ripping it wide open as easy as wet paper. She wonders to herself, "Why does this hurt so bad? Why can't I just quiet my heart?" She knows the answer is because she is betraying her soul, but she searches to try to find and fabricate other reasons to justify the agony in her heart and head. "You don't know me. You don't know me!" she faintly cries. A tear rolls over her face like morning dew on a delicate rose opening from its first touch of light. The man feels the drop of her tear on his shoulder. He begins to wonder if maybe it's true, that she may not be like the rest of them. "What is your name?" he asks in a tender tone. "Cassidy," she whispers. "That's an old name," he says. "You have no idea," replies Cassidy relaxing her stance with an exhale. He replies back to her, "I'm Mr. White. Alistair White."

Cassidy puts her blade back in her stirrup. As soon as he hears the weapon put away Mr. White turns around his swivel chair to face her. She sees a handsome man seated in front of her however, seemingly so fragile to her almost like a different species. "Cassidy, do you know why the Magician wants me replaced?" Mr. White asks her. "Of course I do. The Magician will ceaselessly conquer for more power. A Sisyphean journey of his. Anything and everything his darkness can consume it will. A never ending appetite," says Cassidy as she lowers her head, "I am a prisoner and servant to him now. Hundreds of years ago he made me immortal but only to leave me trapped in purgatory and isolation. Until recently I was liberated from that entrapment. He made me a deal to be freed from the pain of isolation yet into a deeper trap of slavery. I am sorry but words cannot illustrate or do any justice to what I have journeyed. However, surprisingly I see I still have some mercy left. I can tell you surely there is no good deal with the devil. He is a sword in which all sides will inevitably cut."

"I don't understand. Where have you been exactly?" asks Mr. White. "Myself, the Magician, and most of his crew well, we were originally a circus act in a town lost far into the desert now. A freak show of sorts I guess however, life was good. On a fateful night everything changed. Out of rejection of my love he trapped me indefinitely in the town under his spell. He slaughtered everyone and spared only who agreed to eternal life with him. Immortal we are but at the fare of the dominion of our souls. I was released from my entrapment and isolation from the past couple hundred years recently. Under a strict spell I am able to only leave at night returning upon sunrise, and as a servant to him," Cassidy says. She then starts to walk away to admire the family photographs he has on the wall in his bedroom. He notices her deeply looking into the photographs like a poor and hungry child looking into a restaurant. "Cassidy. What if you are the break in the dam to cause the flood. A catalyst to stand for something different. A new illumination for many."

Cassidy knows what he says feels right but there is so much fear and doubt present in her. "That sounds like a wonderful story Mr. White. A glorious one indeed if I was freed, but what good is the brightest of light to the world if it is trapped in the darkness like a sun buried beneath the earth? I can't apprehend the ramifications of betrayal to him. In fact I do not even know what will happen to me now that I could not complete my task tonight," Cassidy replies. She starts realizing all the consequences that lay before her for not doing as she was told and anxiety builds. "What if this is your breaking point Cassidy? The pivotal moment and turn in the road. It's always up to you. Grasp this moment for this is your silence between the music. If there is anything I can do to help let me know. I mean, you obviously know where to find me," White says to her.

Cassidy absorbs what he says accepting the outcome of the night and turn of events as she now begins to worry of the safety of this mortal man. "I'm afraid you need to have ultimate protection from this moment onward. Everywhere you go, and even then you'll be very lucky to stay alive," she says to him. "I will make the calls now," he says as he pulls out his phone and begins to reach contacts. Cassidy proceeds to walk out of the room and before reaching the door White says to her, "You know, I saw something out of my back window before you arrived. I felt something or someone was watching me but at a closer look it was just a large raven." Cassidy stops with introspection and looks over her left shoulder. She immediately thinks of the raven she has been seeing at her home. "Thanks for letting me know that," she says in deep thought and exits the room.

Cassidy leaves the mansion and heads over to her motorcycle noticing Slinger across the street waiting for her. She walks over to him and says with a loud and upset whisper, "What are you doing here? Are you crazy!" Slinger leans forward with one arm resting on his handlebar, "I knew you wouldn't be able to do it Cassidy. I know you girl, too damn well," he says with a slight grin. "Ugh, what is going to happen to me now?" she says rubbing her hand over her forehead and cringing forward with a twisted and upset stomach. "I think you just set sail on a new ship that's all sweetheart. Why don't you just go enjoy yourself the rest of this blessed night before heading home. I'll stay here behind the scene and make sure all is safe. I will also drop you any unfolding details. I got your back Cassidy. You know that. I always have and always will," says Slinger to her as he lifts himself up off the bike to embrace her. Cassidy smiles and gives Slinger a warm comforting hug in return. She feels elated like she never has before and says to Slinger, "I guess sometimes breaking the rules is the most moral thing one can do."

CHAPTER 5

THE POET AND BARDS

While sitting on her bike and starting the engine she takes out of her pocket the flyer she grabbed from the window on her way out of the clothing store. "936 South Street," she says to herself looking at the paper flyer. This place seems so interesting and intriguing to her like an irresistible attraction. Lured to the location she puts the paper back in her pocket and begins to drive rapidly through the city. Throughout her drive Cassidy reflects on the night she was in the store and how kind the old woman was to her. Eagerly turning the corner onto South Street she can see the night cafe in the distance like a warm comforting fire amongst a cold and dark seemingly dead road. Quickly arriving at the location Cassidy parks across the street looking at the warmly lit building and can hear people pleasantly chattering over the live music with a heavy string bass.

Timidly yet anxiously entering the cafe Cassidy sees several small tables with people enjoying one another's company while watching a small stage full of live musicians playing their instruments. While amused by the captivating music she notices a small empty table for one in the very back corner dimly lit with one overhead light gently cascading onto the dark table and chair. Cassidy is magnetized to sit there and to witness what joys this place has to offer. She is deeply intrigued for this is her first night out in so very long to just enjoy life. She knows she is breaking his rules but she feels safe for this brief moment in time or the absence of it and within the capsule of this environment. This new world of people is the likes of what she would have never imagined.

The musicians on the stage finish their last song and people happily applaud. A much older woman with long grey hair, piercing blue eyes, and a face of wisdom enters the stage as the musicians begin to remove their instruments and bring onto the stage a Celtic harp. The older woman announces, "Our next line up of artists for this evening ladies and gentleman will be our dear poets. The precious souls who can eloquently speak of the mysteries of life." The old woman smiles as her piercing eyes graze over the audience and catch in a brief embrace with Cassidy's eyes. "Offer a round of applause for our lady, Miss Brigid," the woman proudly says. The people applaud as a beautiful young woman walks onto the stage holding a small leather notebook. She has long copper hair and warm eyes to match. Brigid sits beautifully with her flowing garments running over a simple stool in the center of the stage. The older woman begins to play the harp and Brigid begins to recite her first several poems about the charms of heaven and the wandering of souls. In the meantime a waiter kindly asks Cassidy if she would like a drink. Cassidy taken aback asks for, "Anything warm," she says to the young man. Embarrassed a bit, she doesn't know what people drink these days or even how to order, and all she knows is her palette for once is inclined to crave a warm restoring drink. The waiter smiles and says to her, "I got you beautiful." He heads off and the poet begins her

next poem. "This next poem is called, 'Raven,'" announces
Brigid.

"Oh great Raven
you set me free
understanding all the deep dark mysteries that be
Oh great Raven
now I can see
a tunnel of vision I have the key
Oh great Raven
you showed my path
Oh great Raven
I am free Alas!"

Cassidy is suspended by this poem and all ceases into the
silence of satori for an expanded second outside of time. It
whispers to her eternal heart. She feels an intense sensation
through her body like a serpent through her spine and knows
something feels more alive than ever before. Speechless still, the
waiter arrives with her drink. "Enjoy," he says setting it on the
table, "I made it special just for you." The harp continues like
warm rain gently trickling through the hollow spaces in the air
bringing solace to the soul. Cassidy picks up the drink
appreciating the treasure she holds in her hands. She closes her
eyes as warm milk glides through her and permeates what
seemed like cold and agitated parts of her being now beginning
to warm. She slowly finishes her drink pondering the poetry of
the raven. Once finished with her drink she drops her payment
on the table of three golden coins and rushes in an attempt to
leave. She knows she doesn't have long at this magical time of
the night and people unknowingly seem to crowd in her way

delaying her. Upon her attempted departure through the crowd the poet speaks her last poem for the night. "That Moment," says Miss Brigid.

"I stared in the face of the misshaped moment
and the tears of my betrayal shaped that moment.
I lived for a short time to see what had transpired
a glutton I am and the devil I had hired.
I stand behind the clock of God
all I can do is say yes and nod.
I turn the dials back and fourth
time stands still the devil's curse.
I eat my hands so they can hold my heart
there's nothing left but a severed part.
I swallow my eyes to see what's inside
a dark empty universe void of my pride.
I will stay in here until all my wows
are slain by my revenge to all my foes.
I eat my tongue and swallow my tooth
until I can give the devil my truth."

Cassidy is overwhelmed at the synchronicities and of the words that penetrate her soul. She shakily pushes through the crowd and departs out of the warm building immediately bursting back into the cold dark street. She starts her engine and rushes down into an isolated alley nearby. Pulling into the darkness of the alley she gets off the bike quickly only to collapse down onto her knees in the humbling weakness of transformation bursting into overflowing tears. It has all been too much for her in one night. Too much to understand and too much stirring in her spirit. Crying next to a dumpster in this small dark alley there is old golden floor lamp with the top light fixtures shaped like a trident placed out by the dumpster to be thrown away. Cassidy looks up at the top of the golden lamp only to notice a raven perched on top the center prod. Cassidy and the raven gaze into each others eyes as the raven penetrates her mind inviting her to rebirth. She is locked into what seems a lucid trance and unable to move.

The unplugged lamp then turns on shining its light brilliantly in the dark. Feeling she surely must be hallucinating now, what appears to be a woman cloaked in black with a dark hood steps before her from nowhere standing in the light. This mysterious woman is only all bones and stands with a monarchial presence. Cassidy strangely unterrified because of a foreign familiarity asked this woman, "Why are you only bones?" The woman replies, "Because bones are the truth." Cassidy's vision begins to blur as she tries to keep focus observing the woman before her. "Surrender and receive emancipation," the woman says sternly. Cassidy almost unconscious can only slightly nod her head, "Yes," she says aloud while still on her knees. Her eyes roll back to close and Cassidy then falls flat on the ground and into blackness.

DAWNING OF STRENGTH

Peering through the cracks in her eyelids Cassidy gradually sees she is home on her bed and the sun's gift of daylight peers through her window. She tries to slowly sit upright with her head spinning back into reality. "Cassidy what happened to you in that alley?" Slinger asks. She looks over to see Slinger sitting in her chair observing her with concern. "I don't know really. Let me get my head on straight first," she replies still trying to sit upright. "Well I found you face down unconscious in an alley. I hitched you on my bike and brought you here, just in time. I hope you didn't go wild again girl," says Slinger. "No...no it's not that," Cassidy says as she begins to remember glimpses of what had transpired last night, "There was this woman...and this, this raven." "What are you talking about Cassidy?" Slinger asks. "Wait, before that the cafe. Then the poet and the harp. That poem and the drink," says Cassidy putting together the events now seeing them in her mind. "I don't know what your mumbling about but we have to think of an alibi to tell the Magician. Or a heck of a good song and dance," says Slinger. Cassidy sighs, "Ugh, I just couldn't do it ya know. His family and the children. The love in his home I felt, and when I heard of the death of his wife I knew it was the Magician. It infuriated me, the suffering he spreads like a disease." "Well what are you going to tell him?" asks the Gunslinger. "The truth," she replies with a smirk. She thinks of the woman made of bones, "Yup. I will tell him the stone cold truth." Cassidy gets up and walks over to her mirror looking at herself realizing how different she appears and says, "I am surely not the person I was yesterday."

Cassidy heads over to her full length mirror in her bedroom. Her long hair is brighter than ever and her sharp windows peak stands out strikingly along with her fierce black eyebrows. Cassidy's keen and now spirited eyes seem more golden than ever before. Stepping back and observing her figure she also sees she is stronger and yet more seductive looking. Slinger then stands up, "Alright lady, I am heading back into town. I'll see you there and I'll admit I am dreading what might transpire tonight. You know I care about you Cassidy," says

Slinger. She turns around to face him, "I know you do, but we both know life as it is can not continue like this. Somehow something along the way has to change it. A catalyst," replies Cassidy. "I just thought we would have an actual plan by then," says the Slinger in distress. "Maybe we just have to let the plan unravel in front of our eyes," she says. "See you there tonight Cassidy," he says and heads out the lonely old building.

The sound of his motorcycle starts noisily in such a quiet area of solitude. Hearing the bike ride off for nearly one minute in the desolate dry dirt Cassidy just stands contently still observing herself in the mirror and listens to the departure until returning back to silence. She then tilts her head in contemplation and walks over to a large ancient looking trunk stored in her room. Brushing dust off the top she remembers opening this trunk so many years ago for her performances and she pauses to reflect about the amazing acts she could do with so many different weapons. The sounds of cheering and joy from the audience still brings a smile to her face at this very moment. She was someone that people liked and were in awe of who she was. She always felt like a hero up on stage performing. With a large sigh Cassidy reopens her heart and then decides to open the trunk slowly and it creeks from age and neglect. Inside lay some of the most beautiful weaponry from so many cultures and eras still glistening with enchantment. Some weapons over thousands of years old and from legends and warriors whose days have passed long ago. She realizes it was her depression for so long that made her not want to look at things that once brought her such happiness and reminded her of such fond days. Now she begins to understand why she was trained to be and is a master at such sophisticated arts of weaponry and combat. It's all for who she is becoming. Who she is now. Or who she has always truly been.

Cassidy's eyes are filled with passion as she takes out her favorite double blades from the trunk. They are alluring broadswords detailed to perfection with an essence of sovereignty. As she holds them in her hands she feels a surge of power vigorously permeating her being. She dances fiercely with her swords around her room and lets the spirit of them captivate her reality. The spirit of fire comes to life and the now blazing noon sun fuels all her aspirations. Cassidy grabs the attachments to holster her double swords behind her back. She attaches them behind her and practices drawing her weapons once again until she feels sublime perfection. She then double checks all her smaller blades attached down her leg and smaller ones in her boots. While double checking her pistols and ammo she realizes her long hair could get tangled within all the weaponry. Heading back over to her mirror Cassidy decides to then braid her hair back in a single streamline french braid tight and secure. She is pleased with it and the way she looks and she subtly smiles at herself in the mirror. She is starting to like who she is again.

CHAPTER 6

THE MIRROR

"What do you mean she didn't kill him!" shouts the enraged Magician. He forcefully stands up kicking his chair back and grabs his dark red embellished cane from beside him. In front of him fearfully stands the Illusionist, Gunslinger, and Fakir. The Magician yells at them all, "One of you knows what is going on around here and someone better tell me now! Thou shalt not break the code and order!" He swings his cane across the table in front of him and all of the glasses full with red wine fly across the room crashing into the white wall. "So tell me. Does anyone know where Mr. White is currently?" he asks. The Illusionist and Fakir look at each other knowing they warned the Magician about Cassidy and understand whomever speaks of it will likely be met with tyranny.

The Gunslinger courageously decides to speak, "He now has full secret service security. Not only around his house but everywhere he goes. It is nearly impossible to get to him now." The Magician's fist tightens around his cane. "Ah! She betrayed me!" he yells and begins to pace around the three men in deep thought. The Gunslinger then sighs and says, "Maybe she wasn't betraying you. Maybe it was just too much for her to handle. I mean you have had her do a lot since you released her." "And you!" The Magician says pointing his finger while walking up to Slinger with penetrating eyes. "I have my eye on you Slinger! I see the way you watch her. You care and do not deny it to my face. Your fondness has my eye in vexation and my tongue in uncertainty. I'm beginning to speculate who you serve," the Magician says to Slinger as he steps right in from of him. The Gunslinger wholeheartedly replies, "Is that really a question after all these years of loyalty? I've only been running around hell's half acre for you since your day of judgment."

The Illusionist speaks up to ease the Magician and calmly says, "I will get more information for you sir about Alistair White. As well on the best ways we can implement execution and secure your replacement. I assure you lord it's nothing we can not handle." The Magician then quiets and calms himself down a bit knowing his loyal Illusionist is always successful. He sits back into his chair and rests his cane in front of him with both gloved hands atop. "What about Cassidy? I have to consider options of consequences for her betrayal. Maybe I will just make her complete her mission. That ungrateful child I will just force her. I can lay out her options for her," the Magician says. The Illusionist replies, "If you give her another chance she may fail again. Who knows what conversation was spoken between the two or what had really transpired. Do you really want to put that level of trust in her again?" The Magician looks at the Illusionist with insight, "Your absolutely correct. The proper replacement of that position is key in my plan of total domination. It is far to important. We will eliminate Mr. White ourselves. Let the town see how powerful and omnipotent we really are. No more hiding our magic. Thank you, and yes find me what you can before we proceed." The Magician in deep thought then looks behind him over his shoulder, "While you are at it I have something I want you to bring with you."

The Magician walks over to a mirror on the wall behind him. It is an enchanting mirror with the frame made of twisting golden vines. He waves his hand over the mirror reciting an incantation intensely into it three times "LA' ATZU WARDUM AMARU INA ANNU! 'Spirit World Slave See Through This!'" He breaths out deeply and smoke seeps out of his mouth as he gently blows it over the mirror. The glass then darkens like the deepest blue of the ocean's unknown waters. He then carefully wraps it in fine silk cloth and gives orders to the Illusionist, "Infiltrate yourself into his home and place this mirror preferably where he sleeps. I want to see if there is further encounters of Cassidy with Mr. White and what they might entail. For we look into the mirror to know thyself yet we shall also look into the mirror to know thy enemy."

The Illusionist graciously takes the mirror honoring his task and swiftly leaves in a black van. He drives through the city to Mr. White's residence following orders without question as always. Once arriving to White's mansion he parks across the street and down aways remaining unnoticed as he takes the time to carefully analyze all the men who go into and out of the property as there are many agents surrounding the premises. He observes that Mr. White's mansion has an extensive gate around the entire perimeter surrounding an exquisite garden so the Illusionist begins to weigh his options of entry. He looks back at the odd mirror and thinks what a task of trickery he has at hand to enjoy. Within moments out front of the entry gate gather several black suited agents discussing amongst themselves. The Illusionist noticing this collaboration sees them gesture to others scattered about to enter. One of the men shouts to another agent across the street, "Come on! Let's go now!" Hearing this the Illusionist jumps on the opportunity for entry. He grabs the mirror and exits the van and within a matter of precisely two seconds he transforms his whole appearance. He clones himself with perfection to the agents image to every detail of attire. Looking at the mirror again he quickly decides to turn the mirror into a briefcase as other agents hold briefcases as well.

Rushing across the street to the men he shouts in an American accent, "Wait! Wait! Sorry I'm late fellas." The agents look back at him with curiosity but quickly shrug it off because of his impeccable disguise. "Alright lets go," says the lead agent as he enters the code to enter the gate. They all enter the mansion and promptly spread out knowing their exact assignment. Some immediately begin setting up microphones and others are inspecting anything and everything. The Illusionist then discretely heads upstairs looking for the master bedroom. One of the other agents on the way says to him, "What are you looking for? Were you not briefed on the premises?" The Illusionist caught off guard replies, "Oh, I had a late night with a special someone to be honest. Priorities man didn't get much of the briefing." The agent replies, "It's alright man I totally get you. I'm too tired to be here myself." The Illusionist chuckles with him playing it off casually, "Well, I will get started with setting mics in the bedroom," says the Illusionist. "Alright, catch ya later man," says the agent as they separate.

The Illusionist proceeds to finds White's bedroom. He enters and closes the bedroom door behind him. Finally alone he lets the briefcase begin to convert back into the mirror in his hands as he searches the room for the best place to hang the mirror. He decides to place it on the wall across from the foot of White's bed positioning it to be viewing the whole room in its entirety as the Magician requested. After placing it on the wall suddenly someone enters the room. It is Mr. White. He walks over looking at the mirror oddly and asks, "Why a mirror? and why such a strange mirror? I mean, it sure is beautiful though like something out of a fairy tale." White then runs his hand along the golden vines on the mirror entranced with fascination. The Illusionist replies, "Sir. I am ordered to use this mirror as a disguise for our mics for your protection. There was no other place in your room where the mics could pick up full audio. Make sure this mirror remains exactly right here for your safety." "Oh. Umm okay, I understand," says the exhausted Mr. White in pure trust. White is obviously overwhelmed and just heads straight to sit atop his bed and loosens his tie. "Have a good day sir," says the Illusionist as he exits. "You too. Thank you," White replies.

The Illusionist exits the house and briskly walks past the gate back to his black van. He starts the engine while looking at his impeccable appearance and drives off. Turning the first corner he morphs back into his authentic appearance. He then calls the Magician, "It's done," he says. "Okay, wonderful," replies the Magician, "Anything you noticed?" he asks. "His mansion is swarmed with protection. As far as anything about Cassidy there was nothing for me to find yet," replies the Illusionist. The Magician then hangs up and walks over to another mirror he has that is exactly identical to the one just placed in Mr. Whites's bedroom. He recites his incantation again, "LA' ATZU WARDUM AMARU INA ANNU." The mirror in front of him manifests a dark hand of a spirit acknowledging his request. The spirit hand gestures in presentation to reveal a crystal clear image of Mr. White's room. He can see the mortal man laid atop his bed passed out and fully clothed. The Magician smiles and is satisfied as always with the Illusionist's work.

Hours pass and Mr. White awakens dismayed to see he passed out atop his bed through the night in suit and tie. He sits up and rubs his tired face while looking at the unusual new mirror in his room. "It's so beautiful," he thinks to himself acknowledging the antiquity and design. It's meticulous and elaborated gold artistry are nothing of this era. He is drawn to walk over to it and he looks deeply into the mirror at his tired face. A shadow passes over the mirror yet unnoticed to his eyes. The Magician stands in his mansion looking right back into Mr. White's face through his identical mirror. They stare into each others eyes engaged with hidden premonitions of dichotomy. The Magician grasps he feels a strong resentment toward Mr. White far surpassing his usual foes but nonetheless cannot identify just yet why. However the Magician knows to have upmost credence to his instincts.

FOR THE WORLD TO SEE

Mr. White's phone rings, "Yeah?" he answers. "Good morning Mr. White. Are you ready for your public announcement at the City Hall today?" says a man on the other line. "I..uhh..umm.. You know what I am running a bit behind," Mr. White replies as he starts taking off his suit in a scramble. "No problem sir. We will pick you up in sixty minutes. Is that okay?" the man on the phone asks. "Yes that's fine," Mr. White says and hangs up abruptly. He then rushes into the bathroom to start his shower.

The Magician watches and listens carefully to the conversation through his spirit mirror. Once watching White hang up the phone the Magician then exits his room and heads down to the grand foyer where his loyal team anticipates his briefing. The Illusionist, Fakir, and Gunslinger await his presence. "We got him. He will be speaking out front of the Los Angeles City Hall in a couple hours. It will be easy to take him out there," says the Magician in assurance and determination. "In front of everyone? The public?" asks the bewildered Gunslinger. The Fakir agrees and says, "There will be live cameras everywhere. Not just the news but people recording all over social media. Are you sure?" "Exactly, it will be perfect. This city needs to see our untouchable power. Our forbidden light is to be revealed to all. Let it spread throughout the world," the Magician replies. "What about Cassidy?" asks the Illusionist. "Forget about her for now. I will deal with her later. She is most likely hiding in fear and cowardice."

The Fakir gets into the drivers seat of his ghostly hearse and the Magician sits down into the passenger seat resting his cane beside him. The Illusionist and Slinger get into the backseats and they all navigate throughout the city in silence with eyes hidden behind dark shades. Their presence entwines through the city streets leaving a lingering aroma of dread behind them. People know who they are and turn a blind eye for they fear any encounter whatsoever with them and the atmosphere dampens as their presence rolls through.

They arrive at the City Hall and a large crowd is already present and awaiting for a historic speech. The media waits anxiously for Mr. White to exit the building for his announcement to the public. Before exiting the hearse the Magician observes the public crowd in contemplation and turns to say to Slinger, "You know, to settle my curiosity once and for all, I would really fancy watching my honorable Gunslinger for assassination today. No one who ever walked this earth has an aim and eye like you. Make me proud today Slinger." The Gunslinger listens and nods keeping all of his rampaging thoughts behind an admirable poker face. He panics inside hidden under his composure as he exits the vehicle visualizing the assassination and shuts the car door. "What will Cassidy think of me if I follow through? If she couldn't do it there must have been a very good reason why," he thinks to himself. He looks back to nod again at the Magician as he walks to position himself on the far right side of the building. He knows the Magician is on to him and his inner strife and he knows today is the day he must decide what winds to embark on for grey deems not to be a worthy road as it leads nowhere and yet forever.

The Magician positions himself across the building on the opposite side of Slinger with the Fakir by his right side. He says to the Fakir, "I know Slinger will fail in his task. That's why I appointed him. At the right time follow me." The Fakir looks at the Magician in a voiceless agreement. The Illusionist makes his way within the crowd as the Magician had ordered him to.

They all serenely anticipate the commotion and turmoil that is yet to unfold bluntly to the world. Mr. White finally makes his way out exiting the front doors of the City Hall and straight to a podium arranged for his speech. He appears tired and bothered yet takes a large inhale and sips water before beginning, "To the people. There has never been such a grave time in our history filled with eminent attacks continuously throughout our major cities with a special concern over our beloved Los Angeles. Simply put this is a coup d' etat. A seizure of power by a rebellious and notable dark force. The tyranny won't just stop here as it will surely spread throughout the country and consuming throughout the world. We must stand strong to protect our loved ones and the simple beauty of our lives. For once darkness bribes its way though the fabric of our communities what's gone will have passed by from the unrighteous and the cowardly. Our special forces are now ordered to come forth with the next barrage of protection for we are surely at war. Now is a time in our American history where we as individuals must choose a side. To conclude within the depths of your own soul if you walk on the alluring side of darkness or walk the righteous path and battle toward the side of light."

The media rushes in to shout over each other at him asking question after question shoving the microphone as close as they can get toward him. One woman asks, "How will this stop the rise of crime?" Another asks, " Can you give us a better answer on the next plan of action?" A man in the crowd also asks, "Do you think any of us can really change the outlook on the future of our city and the future of our people?" Mr. White raises his hand to silence them as much as he can. He leans forward to answer the last question, "Yes, I do. I do believe that the smallest of good deeds, the spirit of integrity, and honor for humanity can lift all out of the darkest of hours toward a new dawn and a new day." White then signals to the crowd that he is finished and he speaks once again to clarify closure so he can just go home, "Thank you for..."

Bang! Rings the sound of a loud gunshot over the people. The crowd is silent with dead air as all absorb the reality of what just ensued. The media backs up alarmed to see White is shot in the left arm. Blood starts permeating through his light grey suit and the sound of his heart beat thuds louder than the lingering ring of the gunshot. He collapses on the ground disoriented and the rushing surge of blood pulls him into unconsciousness. Cameras still roll and the dismayed people scream and panic in complete pandemonium for they are fearful that they too are under attack. The Magician across the way glares at the Gunslinger locking eyes through the chaos knowing he had missed on purpose. Slinger cannot deny anything of his action. He just stands starring back knowing trouble from the Magician is now clearly imminent and a new path was carved for him in that fateful gunshot.

The Magician not wanting anyone to leave the scene exhales a thin and sheer smoke amongst the crowd to sedate the public. He wants the execution shown to the world to prove the new right of power. The people unknowingly inhale the the light mist of smoke and begin to rapidly slow down until halting to a temporary immobility. Within moments the now muted people are swaying about and are incapable of progressing forward in any direction. Inside the people are still in total panic but the only movement they are capable of is watching the rest of the show.

As the Magician and Fakir begin walking their way up to the unconscious Mr. White through the sedated crowd a swarm of officers pull up to the perimeter and secure the area immediately. The Illusionist knowing this is his task starts to make his way over to quickly subjugate the police. As he makes his way to the police he begins to multiply himself with the progression of every step. There must be at least forty five identical shells of himself and yet where the real one is now no one knows. All of his multiple forms stand in front of all the vehicles forming a shield. Officers draw their guns on command but know this magic is not in the realm of what any mortal man should fight and they halt any attack.

WATCH THE SUNSET RISE

Clouds in the sky part revealing the luminous high noon sun in the sky. The Magician and Fakir are now standing over the unconscious Mr. White. With levitation the Magician lifts White up into the air with White's chest high facing the sun. All watch and record in awe and apprehension. The Magician then speaks proudly to the people and the cameras, "Today is the day a new world and beginning commences for everyone. I Samael Sahar the Magician promise everyone a new life under my dominion and command. Walk with me and never look back." He pulls out his ancient and esoteric copper Egyptian dagger. The Fakir kneels down on one knee bowing his head in ceremony. The Magician then holds his shining copper blade high toward the sun shouting his invocation, "ASAR! SAMSUM UTU! 'All seeing eye, power in the sun!'" The captivating sunlight hits the ancient copper blade as it is pierced high into the sky. The Magician lets the dagger float up into the air in suspension out of his hands above Alistair White. All await in complete silence and dismay. The dead air is motionless as time is sealed and all breathing pauses.

Dashing in front of the sun a black movement casts a shadow over the land and the people. Everyone looks up to the eclipse for it is Raven hovering in front of the golden sun expanding and flapping her enormous majestic wings. All are in awe at seeing the silhouette of this stunning and imperial winged being dance in the light.

She darts with miraculous light speed down to the Magician and Mr. White. The Magician's eyes are wide in wonderment and enmity. "It can't be!" he says aloud, "She broke the spell!" Fire rushes through his veins with overwhelming thoughts of betrayal and jealousy. Raven close enough now grabs the copper dagger from the air and lands right in front of the Magician proudly standing face to face with him. He observers her sovereign transformation and her grand shining black wings. "Cassidy. Why did you betray me?" asks the Magician. "I was betraying myself. I am now who I am destined to be. Fear me for I have found myself! I am no longer the shell I once was. That shattered. I am the eternal soul I have always been of the light. As a bearer of the light I now fearlessly shine in dark places no man dares to go," says Cassidy the woman who is now the Raven. The Magician has to accept she overcame his spell and that the battle of duality is inevitable. "So war then commences my love. Fear me! For I have always been and always will be!" announces the Magician. They lay fixed into each others eyes momentarily with polarity. Raven then grabs ahold of the weak and bloody Mr. White. Partially conscious now White looks at the blurred visage of her not recognizing the wondrous creature he sees. She jumps high into the air with him in her arms and flies away into the now bright sky over the horizon.

With shock and revision of reality rippling through the people the Magician staggers back in stupor and outrage. "How did she do it?" he asks himself, "She transcended my spell! Never in all of my existence has this happened. I knew of who she was destined to be but it was supposed to be with me!" The Magician boils with despair and heartbreak. He curls his hands inward and hides his face as his eternal soul cries in loss like the pains of releasing a child into the world forever. His deep emotions of thrashing water causes the earth to rattle and dark clouds to roll in over the city of chaos hiding the light from the world. In this breaking moment of reality the elements above release a downpour of rain in the catharsis of inevitable change. Lightening strikes down to the earth from the heavens shattering expectations. For there is no pain like the wanting of what time has already changed.

The Magician is no longer able to have the eyes of the people see him the maker and the doer humbled by divine decree. He recklessly slashes his cane across the crowd of the people and they fly back and away from him like dead leaves picked up by fall's first gust of wind. He leans back and yells into the sky with a shattering sound saturating the city with his despair. "Cassidy, oh Cassidy! You cannot fathom the forces you stand against!" yells the Magician, "You may think you are free but the heavens have their games too! He then quickly turns around searching for the Gunslinger like a hawk and realizing he is surely gone. "Ahhh Slinger, the gifts I bestowed unto you. You traitor! I knew your soul was divided and now your breach of loyalty has its written consequences. I will find you Slinger only to be fed to the hungry void."

The Magician's eyes light up with fire behind his dark glasses. He then clenches his fist and the building before him begins to crumble flat to the earth. He watches the building collapse as he lifts his hat to run his fingers through his dark hair. The Magician places his hat back on and says in observation, "Mortal men are crushed as easily as their mortal buildings." Turning around he sees the Fakir and the Illusionist faithfully waiting for him by the car and he acknowledges it is time to go and things are the way they are. He walks with his cane calmly toward them with destruction laid behind him. The Fakir opens the door for him and he seats himself inside. "New plans commence, for the time has finally come," announces the Magician as the engine starts. They drive home without conversation and without Slinger back to the Magician's mansion.

CHAPTER 7

THAT WHICH DWELLS IN THE UNDERWORLD

Cassidy who is now the Raven carries Mr. White through the air in her arms back to his home. She lands in the back of his mansion and her wings begin to vanish as she walks forward through the lush trees. Unheard she carries him inside the mansion to his room as the grandfather clock strikes three p.m. and she lays him gently onto his bed. White opens his eyes to see her refreshing face and adoration flushes over him. She looks back into his eyes with deep compassion and they embrace in a muted conversation of the soul for just one suspended second. Abruptly several secret service men burst into the room disquieting a very harmonious moment. With their firearms drawn and fright trembling in their eyes at her presence, "Get down now!" the lead agent yells at her. The dazed Mr. White knows Cassidy is a good soul yet he is still only half conscious and just beginning to become aware of his surroundings. "No!" White tries to yell in his state of weakness. He feels awful he doesn't have the strength to shout his command to cease fire. One, two, three, four, five shots are fired into her abdomen as she begins to try to speak of her change of heart. The last gunshot echoes throughout the quiet house and silence overtakes them all as Raven remains standing.

Blood trickles down to her feet but she is unbothered and unfettered. "Why do you attack me yet you not know of my mission?" Raven asks the men. The agents lower their guns knowing their attacks are futile. "She's a…she's a good one," Mr. White whispers with effort. This touches one of Cassidy's most tender wounds of past afflictions. Containing her amazement of her melting wounds inside her soul she looks at him with an ever so slight grin. She then reaches to his injured arm and rips open the fabric revealing to him he has been healed. "My God," Mr. White says as he is bewildered seeing smooth healed skin and yet clothes full of blood. White then looks to Raven's stomach that is now almost completely healed. "Am I immortal too?" he asks. Raven chuckles, "No, I am afraid you don't want that burden and responsibility. However I did heal you on our way over here."

"Who are you?" the lead agent asks her. Cassidy begins to answer and stops herself before answering with her formal name. She knows she has transcended into something far different now. Although part of her will always be the Cassidy that always was, she also understands she has evolved into Raven. At this moment she realizes she wants to be a hero and makes her commitment and bond to journey forward as a hero. Someone people will pray to save them. "I am Raven," she replies, "And I will defeat the Magician. I will subdue the evil he trails behind and do my best to transmute the dark path he leaves into something marvelous. A promise of emancipation from tyranny." The agent then asks her, "So are you on our side? The side of the people?" Raven intensely replies, "Yes. Yes I am."

The agent takes out a device out of his pocket that appears foreign to her. He cautiously steps up to her and says, "Raven, my name is Agent Goodwin. Take this device if you will. It is untraceable and safe to use. I hope we will be able to trust and coordinate with you." Raven then takes the device and looks at it foreignly. "This is how you answer, and this is how you can reach us. It's a phone." he says showing her how to use it. He hands her the device and she attaches it onto her belt next to her right pistol. Agent Goodwin reaches out to shake her hand, "To a brighter future for all," he says. Raven shakes his hand in agreement, "Yes," she responds in eye contact. She looks at Mr. White once again and then makes her way to exit the window. Jumping out into the cold air her wings appear again and Raven soars off into the nightfall sky back to her home.

The Magician keenly watches and listens through his mirror and becomes furious with rage. "Get out the giant!" he yells to his men while watching Raven fly out the window. "Get me my Abatu!" The Fakir hastily grabs a large set of keys held on a ring of red jade and runs to a heavy wooden door within the first floor of the mansion. He shuffles through the keys and unlocks the aged door that opens only to a staircase below. The Fakir runs down the long and dark staircase made of stone that is ancient and mystic in its structure. The further down he goes the seven layers below the darker it gets until heading into complete blackness. Out from the utter darkness emerging lights from candle flames light up the bottom of the stairs as he finally enters the seventh realm. Opening the door at the very bottom of this realm all is otherworldly and filled vastly with large arching halls, chambers, and vaults and all is lit golden from the burning flicker of mysterious lights. Large columns support the arches and water trickles down elegantly over some of the stone walls. With halls leading in all directions, some light and some dark and many filled with mysterious heavy doors, the mortal man would be certain to be lost here forever.

Sounds of cries, whispers, and laughter come from behind many of the doors. Some doors several people behind one talking amongst each other. Some doors filled with sorrow and others with cheer but the mystery of what's behind remains sealed with the word. The Fakir arrives to a large door at the end of a tunnel off to the left. He unlocks the door and hears a monstrous moan. Opening the door he sees Abatu the giant sitting peacefully on the floor in his enormous high ceiling cathedral he uses as his room. A glimpse of light peers through a high window of stained glass revealing the chambers reach a source of unknown light and a small bird he was feeding flies away from the sudden opening of the door. "Abatu," says Fakir, "Master needs you now." Abatu stops reading a small book and angrily closes it and throws it on the floor in agitation. "ARRRGHHH!" he replies as his expression of frustration.

Abatu knows he has no choice but to obey. He grabs his giant weapon off the wall which is like a large staff with a grand heavy blade at the top and a spear at the end. He stomps out of his room making miles around him tremble with each step as he drags the heavy weapon on the ground reluctantly following Fakir out of the room. As they walk down the hall they pass a door on the right that cracks open. It is the Puppeteer and he peers through the crack observing and mumbling to himself as they pass. Finally getting all the way back to the top up through the seven layers and to the entry door the Magician awaits him. "Abatu, my Abatu. The best giant in town," the Magician says like it was still the circus days as he kisses his cheek, "We need you Abatu. Show the world, Abatu the Giant!" the Magician shouts in attempt to get Abatu excited to be out of his cave.

The Magician reveals to Abatu and old photograph of the circus. He points to Cassidy in the photo and asks, "Remember Cassidy Abatu?" Abatu nods in agreement and he smiles some as he thinks of fond memories of her and him in performance. The Magician promptly sees this and says, "No Abatu, I am sorry to tell you Cassidy is very bad now. She wants to hurt us and ruin our home." Abatu then looks perplexed and saddened like a child. "Yes I am sorry to tell you Abatu she wants to destroy your master," the Magician says. Abatu drops his head in acceptance and would never question his master. "Also there is this guy Abatu," The Magician says as he shows him an image of Mr. White. "He wants us all dead. He is Alistair White and he is a very terrible man. We need to destroy them both so we can stay a safe family Abatu. Bring Cassidy to me okay. Can you help me?" the Magician asks with pristine acting in sorrow and heartache. Abatu holds and looks at the photographs and seemingly saddened of the news but still loyal to the Magician Abatu replies, "Yes master I will help you."

THE FIRST BATTLE

Cassidy rests in her abode drinking marigold tea while watching the stars outside her window flicker like the sunlight reflecting off water. "It won't be long until the sun rises," Cassidy ponders to herself. She is more peaceful than ever before and feels her heart once again like the first spring after a thousand of the coldest of winters. This love for herself anew brings her more power and strength that is imaginable and she is yet to discover it. She heads happily downstairs to make herself some more tea and her new phone from Goodwin begins to vibrate on the counter. Breaking the moment of bliss she knows it has to be serious. "Hello?" Cassidy says curiously as this is her first time answering a phone. "Hello Raven, this is Agent Goodwin and we have a problem. Something we have never quite seen," he says apprehensively. "What do you mean?" Cassidy asks. "There is what appears to be a giant heading to Mr. White's mansion. I don't know who else is with him but this type of magic is not in the expertise of even our most advanced military. Can you somehow help us Raven?" Goodwin asks her. Cassidy without a blink of an eye replies, "Yes, of course. I will be right there."

Cassidy quickly drinks the last of her marigold tea and then begins to attach on her desired equipment and weapons. Before leaving Cassidy remembers the might of the giant and rummages through her trunk to find her chain and a peculiar nail with a magic emblem atop. With a grin she finds the nail and places it hidden alongside her boot and attaches the chain onto her side. She then steps outside into the empty western town street and the lonely wind passes by on her face. Feeling watched, she looks up to see the ravens perched atop the town clock observing her as they always do. Cassidy smiles and looks up to the starry night sky before propelling herself into the air and magically expanding her magnificent wings. The night light illuminates her face and chest faced high toward the moon. Momentarily she looks down onto the town she was once trapped in and now soars above it. Raven then darts through the dark sky to fearlessly face whatever may come.

The giant Abatu walks heavy footed toward the city dragging his massive weapon behind him. The Magician proudly watching him walk away yells, "Abatu reveal your strength! Let the whole world see!" Abatu the giant then moans as he unfolds to a monolithic size. All he has left on his body after the transformation is red cloth covering his hips. He looks like an ancient giant of legends with piercing green eyes and fiery red hair striking fear in all yet captivating with his beauty and godlike anatomy. His fierce weapon becomes proportionate to his evolved size as well and he continues forward steadfast on the mission.

Agent Goodwin waits inside White's mansion peeking through a front window in panic and awe seeing Abatu heading closer with the earth trembling in each thud of his giant bare feet. Daybreak is near and the birthing light casts an aura on the horizon highlighting Abatu whom was once called, "The blessed giant." People scurry to hide and pandemonium breaks the silence of disbelief. Militarized police are now fully engaged anticipating the arrival out front of White's mansion. Abatu makes it around the last and final corner alas revealing himself confidently to the army in front of him. "Fire!" shouts agent Goodwin. After three seconds of dread and wonderment of his statuesque appearance fire and fury is then engaged toward the giant. He looks down at the insignificant wounds across his body that only begin to infuriate him. Abatu takes his giant left hand and sweeps it across the attacking army launching them effortlessly out of his way.

In an attempt to disable the giant's strength immediately other forces are ordered to use their prepared sonic weapons.

"Now!" agent Goodwin yells, "What are you waiting for!" The sonic weapons are fired and the highly disturbing sound starts to cripple Abatu down to his knees. His yell shakes and ripples through the earth while he covers his ears, "ARRRGHHHH!" he screams and his green eyes light up with fire. Everyone waits in frail hope this will subdue the giant. Abatu with all his might pulls himself upright and up off his knees. Despite the immense pain and agony from the sound he smashes his fist down over and over again onto the sonic weapons obliterating them all and whomever may be in them. He then slowly stands back upright as the ringing pain subsides and he looks down at the obliterated weapons becoming agitated far more so than before. Inside his soul he just wants to get this task over with quickly so he can go back home and be comfortable in his peaceful room with his beloved ancient books. He looks straight forward with determination at the mansion now and begins to sprint straight to his target.

Agent Goodwin has been calling Raven throughout the suspenseful and fearful arrival of the giant without being able to reach her and now with Abatu in full sprint initiating the final attack agent Goodwin yells into Raven's voicemail one last time, "Raven where are you? We need you Raven!" The look on Goodwin's face has changed from fear to acceptance of death. Everyone has given up hope against such an unfathomable power. Abatu has now arrived out front of the mansion and as he towers above it he lifts his massive weapon in the air ready to thrust it down in ultimate destruction over the mansion. The new dawn's sun shines onto the metal blade reflecting its glorious light. Raven at incredible speed flies through the air blocking the weapon just in time hovering in front of Abatu's face. Her two hands grab the staff of the weapon holding back the giant's shining blade now over her head.

Abatu stares at her blankly without an ounce of him recognizing her. "Abatu! It's Cassidy. You need to stop Abatu!" she yells to him in empathy. The giant Abatu quiets his thoughts and remembers the Cassidy he liked so long ago. He looks at her with confusion and suspicion of her transformation. Then he hears the Magician in his ear, "My Abatu Cassidy is bad now. I am sorry but you must destroy her Abatu! Now! Do not trust her!" Abatu becomes heated and twisted with confusion following the Magician's orders out of loyalty and pushing aside pursuits of the soul. He quickly reaches out to try and grab Raven in his huge fist. Raven propels back up to the sky. "ARRGHHH!" Abatu yells again becoming rapidly annoyed and looking up at her like a pest in the sky. Raven knows she doesn't really want to hurt him, for he too used to be her friend. She begins to think of ways to defeat the situation with the least amount of struggle and harm.

Raven then swiftly lands on the ground in front of him crouched low. He looks down on her thinking it shall be an easy defeat. He thrashes his weapon down toward her smashing the thick heavy blade into the earth. To his surprise she effortlessly dodges all of his attacks. Over and over with the continuous efforts the more and more frustrated and exhausted Abatu gets. Raven takes advantage of the open opportunity of his now slow and tired pace and sprints straight forward at him with her long hair tailing behind her. The tired Abatu cannot react in time to Raven's speed yet watches the oncoming attack with a blurred perplexity. Raven darts forward with a a double legged push kick directly into Abatu's chest. So much power comes out of Raven's kick it thrusts Abatu backward making the giant land forcefully onto the ground and rippling the crust of the earth surrounding him.

The people are awestruck by the historic fight and watch in total astonishment at the supernatural. Agent Goodwin picks up his phone to answer a call from the President of the United States. "I think we got it under control now," says Goodwin without taking his bulging eyes off Raven and the giant. He hangs up the phone without listening to the President for he is too aghast witnessing the unearthly to comprehend anything. Raven begins to walk over to the almost defeated giant laying on his back. "Why Abatu?" Raven asks. Abatu hears this and instead of accepting he is up against a force he isn't capable of defeating he still decides to try one more time for his ego is crushed. He turns his giant head to the side to look at her and his blood boils with jealousy of the mighty force she has become. He knows he cannot face the Magician with defeat. Abatu ponders to himself, "How? How did she become so mighty and fearless?"

Abatu then bursts up with his last gust of energy. Forgetting Raven he heads straight back toward Mr. White. Catching Raven in surprise he leaps ahead of her and begins to throw a fierce right fist straight toward the mansion. Raven sprinting after him grabs ahold of his ankle to minimize impact of his fist and pulls him backwards. She strides up the giant's body and he begins to struggle chasing her over his body with his hands to catch her as she moves about. Raven then climbs onto his shoulders and uses her chain to run it around his neck several times before jumping off his back and slamming him hard back down to the ground. Holding the end of the chain she pulls out the large magic nail from her boot and in one slam with her palm she hammers it deep through the earth pinning the chain and the giant down. No ordinary nail it is, it unravels beyond a mile beneath the surface locking an immense and mighty hold. The giant now screams more maddened than ever in his incoherent yells.

Raven backs up away from his flailing limbs. "Abatu! Surrender! I am your friend. You have been lied to Abatu... I can help you!" Raven says in a loud earnest tone. Abatu however is too embittered to listen to her plea. With his immense strength and spiteful face he arrises breaking the chain off the ground. Standing before Raven he grabs the chain tight around his neck with both hands and rips the chain off with a terrorizing scream and pulsating veins flare up through his arms and to his neck. Raven has no other choice but magic. Still not wanting to hurt her former ally she kneels on one knee and thrusts her hands forward toward him. White light emanates out of her hands and penetrates the giant. Starting from the ground up Abatu the giant turns to solid stone. A monolithic rock now stands frozen in time in mid agony and fury.

Raven stays kneeled for a moment to catch her breath. Dirt and dust from the battle begin to settle and she arrises to her feet. She looks up at the statue before her and says to it, "I'm sorry Abatu. I'm so sorry." Slowly people begin to rummage out of hiding and marvel at the wonder before them. Never have they witnessed the supernatural. Agent Goodwin exits the house and unsteadily walks over to Raven. "Raven... You are a hero," he says with reverence in his eyes to her. She turns around to see him and feels a serene bliss inside from hearing those words spoken. They then both turn to see Mr.

White exiting out the front of his mansion. Mr. White's eyes are wide as he looks at the frozen giant standing behind Raven seemingly looking right back at him. "My God..." says White. Tears run down his face as he observes in astonishment. "Raven," he says as he makes his way closer to her. "Raven, you have saved my life. Twice now in fact. You have saved many now Raven," White goes on speaking with continued tears. "No Mr. White. You are the one who saved me," Raven replies with an ever so slight grin while her eyes show peace and gratitude. Her being exudes a genuine contentment. "He won't move. Trust me," she says to Goodwin and White. They both take another look at the harrowing stone towering over them. "Ok Raven, we trust you but we can't say we feel easy inside looking at him everyday," says Goodwin. "Yea, I get to see him every morning now," replies White.

Raven walks away from White and heads over to the stone Abatu. She places her hand on his leg and whispers to him, "Hopefully I can help you Abatu." She then sees his savage and barbarous weapon laid a couple yards away from him. It is back to normal size now and is about the length of her body. Raven picks it up and throws it over her shoulders and launches into the air expanding her glorious wings. She propels off disappearing behind the golden sunlit clouds toward her abode. Agent Goodwin and Mr. White look at each other. "That is one great victory but what is yet to come next?" says Goodwin to White. "No one can ever fathom what can conjure out of the darkness," replies White. They both look at each other in accordance to stay prepared for what is next at hand.

CHAPTER 8

ACE OF SPADES

Raven arrives home to her isolated town. As she lands in the street she hears rummaging coming from the old saloon. She enters the bar slow with curiosity gently pushing open the swinging doors. To her surprise it is Slinger having his way at the old saloon bar helping himself. Without looking back at her he asks her, "Wanna play an ol' hand of blackjack?" Cassidy goes to sit next to him and sighs, "Where have you been? I know you left into hiding after you could not follow the Magician's orders at the City Hall, but where?" she asks. Slinger shuffles his cards a couple times before answering, "I have to keep on the run now little missy. I'm afraid the games have officially begun. I'll be here and there and a little bit of everywhere. You'll see me now and then. Just promise me one thing Cassidy. If he ever uses me to sway you, let your mind and heart not waiver for the greater good is at stake." "We won't let him catch you Slinger. We cannot," Cassidy says as she lowers her head with chills knowing the chambers of the Magician's halls of eternal punishment. "I know what place you're thinking of Cassidy," Slinger replies. "But even if need be I would rather sacrifice myself for the victory of a new and better world." "No!" Cassidy shouts, "Don't even take it there!" She places her hand atop of his and with a sigh a tear falls from her face onto the top of the shuffled card deck. Slinger curiously pulls the card from the top of the deck that her tear anointed. He turns it over to reveal the Ace of Spades. Cassidy and Slinger look at each other briefly without a word. Breaking the silence Slinger asks Cassidy, "Well you still wanna play a round of blackjack? Like we used to?" Cassidy replies, "Hell, after all those years here I only play solitaire now. A game I play by myself and control by myself," she chuckles a little, "When you play by yourself you can cheat a lil' and win. You sure learn a lot in solitude I tell you."

Slinger places his hands around the sides of Cassidy's face. He looks into her eyes like a father with unconditional love and says to her, "Remember what I said Cassidy. Okay? I will be out of here by morning. When I can I will leave you notes. Everything from this point forward is in your hand in your game of solitaire Cassidy, so keep your head and your heart unwavering."

Resting deep in his lair simmering in deep thoughts with a cigar and cognac the Magician sits down shirtless into a red velvet chair. His lean and muscular physique rests back into the luxurious chair complementing his flawless complexion. "I have completely underestimated her," says the Magician to the Illusionist, "We cannot move forward with anything apparently until we subdue Cassidy or Raven, whatever they call her now. Absolutely nothing can be done with her expanding powers." "I'm sorry sir but I reckon I warned you of her," says the Illusionist standing far across the room from him. "I know! I know… It was part of my plan to have her powers with us. The thing is, I have always seen the potentials inside of her. I knew I had to keep her beaten, worn down, and isolated. Mentally and spiritually broken so I could be the one to bring her up and forever have her loyalty. I actually had an affinity for her which I don't know if that will ever subside however it be I confess I am at war with the one I love. My duality, she shines so bright, so illuminated, yet I must destroy her," says the Magician taking a huge inhale and exhale of his cigar.

The Illusionist poised and calmly asks the Magician, "So what will it be next?" Then a mirage of the Illusionist appears speaking behind the Magician leaning into his left ear as the image of him across the room fades away, "I will await your following orders my lord," he says. The Magician gazes off to the left in thought briefly and says, "You need to get her for me. It has to be you. She has too much direct power but her mind isn't as strong as your manipulation of reality. She will mentally crumble. Also find me Slinger's whereabouts. We shouldn't let him wander too far. Eventually we need to capture him for formal treatment of rebellion of loyalty. But first get me Cassidy, she is the priority. You have always been my favorite Raziel." He turns to look at Raziel behind him but now he stands back across the room again. "Thank you my lord," replies the Illusionist as he makes his way out of the room closing the door behind him. The Magician stands up to go gaze at himself in his full length mirror. He undresses completely and admires his sculpted body and ponders in vanity before stepping into his extravagant sauna bath. Sinking in deeper into the bubbling hot water he confidently says aloud to himself, "Raven, oh Raven my love I shall triumph over you and your light like I have always done since the beginning."

TWO KEYS AND THE LIBRARY

The Gunslinger meanders around town on his bike until he feels confident he is not being watched. He rides down a forgotten and lonesome road overgrown with greenery and twisting vines. The stillness in the air here against the slowing rhythm of his motor brings him momentary peace amongst his climbing anxiety. He pulls up to a seemingly abandoned library made of stone and parks hidden in the back. He uses a concealed entrance behind the building covered in ivy to enter unseen into the aged yet sturdy library like he has been here routinely many times before. Once inside there are three directions to choose. One to the left, the right, or straight ahead. He walks down the empty hallway to his right and bypassing the entrance ahead and the hall to the left. He continues down to the end of this hallway until arriving to a plain unmarked door colored in a deep orange like that of a sacred flame. Slinger opens the door and steps into a completely empty room of four walls made of brick stones. Standing in the very center of the room he confidently recites, "AZAG MUDUTU! 'Great Serpent Knowledge!'" Promptly after finishing his incantation an additional door appears in the room on the very wall in front of him. Slinger then pulls out an alluring and beautiful silver key out of his pocket to enter this celestial door marked with cryptic symbols and illuminated emblems. Once he inserts the key and unlocks the heavy mysterious door sounds of water are heard streaming affluently from below. Following the symphony of water he is lead down a small narrow staircase to an underground library.

Like a whole other world this library holds forbidden books of truth, knowledge, legend and lore the world has never seen nor heard before. Everything is beautiful with vast hallways of adorned books from throughout mankind and beyond from the other side. In the middle of the room there is a large sacred tree stump reaching out of the ground to rest upon while reading and absorbing the rivers of knowledge.

Making his way alone through the vast library he heads all the way to the very back. On the bottom right shelf tucked away in the corner is an ancient black book that looks very plain and bare in appearance yet yields an unearthly and intimidating aura. He picks up the book with a trembling right hand and dusts it off. All that is written on the black book cover is four number twos engraved in gold. Slinger opens the book to reveal what he already knew. It is not a book at all but a wooden closure made of yew wood unable to open with no keyhole nor code. Slinger knows what is inside the box within the book and it makes him uneasy to even be handling it. He hides the book in his jacket and swiftly makes his way to exit the secret library. Leaving out the back door covered with ivy he is anxious to get onto his bike and leave the premises. He looks around nervously to make sure he wasn't noticed or followed. Hopping onto his bike he starts the loud engine immediately and blasts off around from the back corner and speeds down the street anxiously to his next stop.

The sun begins to lower bringing a chill in the air and Slinger heads swiftly to White's mansion with the book held tightly in his jacket. He approaches the front gate and the four guards standing out front. Jumping off the bike quickly he heads toward the guards. The men are cautious with Slinger's approach and ready their hands on their firearms. "I am here to speak to Mr. White. It is urgent," says Slinger. "There is no entry from anyone period. I'm going to have to ask you to leave immediately," says one of the guards. "Tell him it's a friend of Raven, and that it is urgent! Please," begs Slinger. "Hey, we got a guy that says he is a friend of Raven and needs to speak to Mr. White," says the guard into his collar microphone. "This is Agent Goodwin speaking. Who is the man? What is his name?" asks Goodwin. "I'm Slinger, the Gunslinger. You know the one that missed and shot Mr. White's arm. That guy," shouts Slinger loudly overhearing agent Goodwin and hoping he can hear him. From inside the guest house on the property agent Goodwin moves the camera located atop the gate to view Slinger from inside. Seeing it is really him Goodwin anxiously responds, "Let him in now!" The guards immediately open the gates for Slinger to enter. He gets back on his bike and drives up the long walkway passing the giant Abatu to his left. "I'm sorry Abatu we will get you out of here soon my friend," he whispers to the stone statue.

He finally steps up to the front door and before he is able to knock Mr. White opens the door. "Sorry bout' your arm," says Slinger quickly before any formal introduction. "That's fine... I uhh. It's all better now. Come inside let's talk," says White. "Sure, I don't have much time," replies Slinger nervously. "Well what is it?" asks White. "There is something of dire importance that Cassidy, I mean Raven receives," he says as he pulls out of his jacket the mysterious black book. He is beyond uneasy revealing the book yet hands it over in good faith. Mr. White takes the black book in his hands looking at its captivating allure and yet simplicity. He runs his hands over the front reading, "2222." "What is this?" asks White "What does this mean?" "I'm sorry I reckon can't answer that question sir," replies Slinger, "Just please make sure it only makes it into her hands."

White then opens the book seeing an aged wooden box made of yew. Trying to open it with might he is perplexed and looks at Slinger in bewilderment. "I really wouldn't bother," says Slinger. Slinger then hands White the beautiful and embellished silver key in a small purple bag with tied drawstrings along with a note in a red wax sealed envelope. "These are of upmost importance she receives as well," says Slinger in sincerity locking eyes with White in a soulful agreement. "I understand," replies White. "Hopefully we can meet again. You're a good and honorable man," Slinger says as he tilts his hat goes to head out the front door. "Wait!" White replies, "I need to know. Do you know what the Magician will strike with next? How should we prepare?" While opening the door Slinger stops and partially turns around to face White with his left eye, "You can't prepare for the dark void, it's like a deck of blank cards. You just gotta play with what you got when it reveals itself." Slinger then pauses for a moment with a sigh and asks, "You like her don't you Mr. White?" White thrown off by the question replies, "I uh, I… I mean she is beautiful. Everyone knows that, but she is beyond out of my league. I mean, she's literally a goddess." Slinger smirks, "Okay," he says and then heads out of the building and gets onto his bike. He revs up his engine and heads back toward the gate and exits the safety of the mansion.

The guards see Slinger approaching and open the gate entry for him to leave. He increases speed as he turns the corner out of the entrance and races down the street vanishing off into the sunset. The guards look at each other in perplexity, "That was odd," says one of the younger guards. "Yeah, things are getting too strange for me to handle these days. What kinda times are we living in?" asks another guard while looking back at the giant frozen statue of Abatu. "Maybe the end of days who knows," replies an older guard while looking at his watch, "On that note I have to get home early tonight folks. Catch ya some other time!" He immediately begins walking away. "Wait! Boss is gonna be pissed. You'll be fired for sure! You can't just leave mid shift!" shouts the younger of the guards. The guard just continues to walk down the street quickening his pace without acknowledging the other guards. He gets into a pickup truck and begins to drive away from the mansion. The guard then looks into his rear view mirror and watches his eyes as they shift back into the Illusionist.

Mr. White gets out his phone and calls Goodwin, "I need to speak to Raven," White demands. "What is going on Mr. White?" Goodwin replies. "I have some critical items that must get safely into her hands and her hands only," White says hastily. "Ok I understand but there is no way it would be safe for you to travel. She must come here to you sir. I will contact her for you," Agent Goodwin replies, "And I will let you know promptly once contact is made." "Thank you agent Goodwin," says White and hangs up the phone. Goodwin instantly contacts Raven texting her, "Raven we need you here at the mansion for very important particular items to pick up."

Raven's eyes peer open from her nap in a dark room lit with oil lamps and hears her phone beep. She sits upright with an inhale and pulls her fingers through her scalp before she walks across the room to look at the phone. She reads the message from Goodwin and takes some time pondering how to message back for she hasn't yet done this before. After fiddling with the device for several minutes she replies back to Agent Goodwin, "When?" she texts. "Sooner the better," replies Goodwin immediately, "In fact we are having a ball this Friday evening at the mansion. Many government and military people favorable to Mr. White will be attending. You are more than welcome to have your presence Miss Raven in fact we would all be honored and it would be a safe transfer of the items. However, you are welcome anytime Raven."

She sets the phone down feeling cold nerves run about in her center surprisingly at the notion of dressing up and attending such an event. She wonders if she can appear refined enough and decorous as she looks across her bedroom at the dress she bought from the gypsy with its captivating exquisiteness enticing her thoughts. She goes over to the gown and holds it in front of her body while gazing into the mirror. She wanders off in her mind imagining herself freely dancing, feeling beautiful and free of any worries. Quickly snapping into the reality that she is truly destined to attend the ball Raven then sets the dress back down and heads to her dresser opening the drawer to reveal the most stunning antique jewelry. She begins arranging her collaboration indulging into a precious moment to embrace her womanly allurement.

CHAPTER 9

WELCOME TO THE CARNIVAL

Raven's clock strikes three a.m. and she instantly hears outside increasingly louder carnival music and sees a colorful array of lights flashing through her window. She heedfully peers out her window to see a carnival house set up just outside the outskirt of her town. "Come and join the fun this evening at the happy happy carnival!" says a circus performer's voice boisterously overtaking the serenity of the lonely desert. "Your fun is our pleasure!" the eerie voice continues on sending an ominous chill through Cassidy. She knows this can't be anything good yet knows there is no way of avoiding this devious plan of the Magician. Before she prepares to head out she stops herself acknowledging the obvious and saying to herself, "It can't be the Magician... It has to be the Illusionist. The Magician would never face a battle without using his best players first." Knowing this she anticipates many of her weapons might deem useless as this will surely be a battle of trickery. However she cannot feel comfortable parting completely from some of her precious blades.

Raven fearlessly walks through the dirt road between the small town towards the carnival house settled on the outskirt.

Four large arrows flashing in red lights point to a small door in front of the carnival house. "Enter here for fun fun fun!" continues the eerie voice. Arriving to the entrance she places her hand on the door handle pausing momentarily and takes several deep breaths. She knows what he is capable of. She has seen him lead the wisest of men to permanent insanity. Opening the door the music becomes increasingly louder sensing her acceptance and arrival. She braces herself and steps her left foot forward inside and hesitant to continue with her right leg yet letting it gradually enter into full commitment. Before she can turn to close the door behind her it is forcefully slammed and locked by an unseen energy. This doesn't waiver her courage for she knows the war is inevitable.

Raven continues forward in the dissolute dark with the happiest of music playing. There is a set of stairs before her with no other direction to go. Proceeding onto the stairs that appear to go upward and after reaching no destination she begins to notice these stairs are taking her yet in fact a downward direction. With each frustrating step up she can't understand what deception is at play. "You're almost there Cassidy," says the voice, "Just a little further." Cassidy continues on and on. It must be hours now or at least it feels like so and she is understanding if this continues she might be too drained for the battle. She comes to a halt and stops any movement on the dark mysterious stairs. "Don't look behind you," says the voice. Cassidy in suspension standing on these stairs that now feel like the empty void of the universe turns around with irresistible curiosity to look behind her. She turns to see all the stairs behind her have completely disappeared. She now stands on the very last stair in the middle of nothingness. The stair begins to tremble making her balance become uneasy, "I said don't turn around!" says the voice angrily now. The stair trembles more and more and Cassidy struggles to hold on. The music suddenly stops to an uncomfortable silence. Without any control nor stability she falls off the last stair into the blackness falling and falling seeing nothing but the dark dark blackness. Suspended in fear she falls for what seems like forever. The fall is so long she begins to wonder if she is even falling anymore and just then she hits the bottom hard. Slowly coming to consciousness she spits blood on the white floor where she lays. As soon as her blood touches the marble it penetrates the floor. It fills up the entire floor in which she lay from a pure white to a now blood red floor. It was only a drop of blood she thinks to herself. She realizes her mind is panicking now and must calm herself the best she can.

She begins to try and stand on the red floor and the sound of a candle being lit makes her whip around in alertness. The whole room then rapidly fills up in candle light creating a circle of light around her. On the outskirts of the candle lights are full mirrors in a circle as well which multiply the effect of the flames of the lights. Looking upward is still the dark black void in which she fell through. Music begins to play again yet now a solo violin. Looking forward she sees in the mirror the reflection of the Illusionist standing behind her. He smiles wide and the smile continues to expand unnaturally through the mirror. She turns around to face him and gets a blow across her jaw almost knocking her out. "Didn't I tell you to not turn around Cassidy?" says the omnipresent voice. Cassidy still standing rolls back with her right cross which seemed to land perfectly but yet he isn't there. She gets countered in the gut sending her straight back.

Now truly appearing directly before her the Illusionist engages in full combat with Cassidy and the violin speeds its tempo. They exchange the most integrate and elaborate combat as they were always the Magician's two best trained fighters and skilled with his sacred knowledge. However the Illusionist is the only one who was taught the Magician's mastery of deception. She flashes back to a time in training under the Magician where they were fiercely jealous of each others skills. She remembers how they locked eyes way back then in envy and suspicion and here they are locked in glare once again. She grasps now what that uncertainty in him really was way back then and questions if this battle was always written.

The raging war between them continues and Cassidy begins to notice there are several forms of the Illusionist appearing within the mirrors around the room. As the violin slows its melody she wonders if the one she fights before her is really him. The Illusionist standing before her then stops all movement and begins to dissipate like dust into nothingness. She stands alone as mysterious winds rolls through the room making the candle flames flicker. She runs over to one of the candles to put it out. She thinks if maybe she takes away the light his illusion of multiple forms it won't distract her as much and she'd be better off fighting in the dark. As hard as she blows on the flame to put it out it doesn't waver.

At that moment Cassidy comprehends not all the flames are real. "Which flame is the real one?" she thinks to herself looking around the room at the circle of fire. She goes from one candle to the next counterclockwise and her subsequent effort deems useless. Cassidy feels she has surely made more than three rounds at least in a circle and not one flame is real.

"But how?" she debates to herself. Her eyes are wide and tremble with the illusions weighing on her sanity. "Do you want darkness Cassidy?" asks one particular reflection of the Illusionist in front of her. Cassidy punches the mirror as hard as she can and a loud crack like an explosion breaks the mirror. She pulls her fist back now watching all the mirrors begin to shatter and collapse to the ground on the outskirt of the candles. Turning around she sees one last mirror standing with the Illusionist inside it smiling. She walks confidently now over to him in eye contact and before a couple feet away he says to her, "Wrong Cassidy!" At that moment the last mirror shatters before her and all the candle lights perish simultaneously. At once the solo string violin ceases to play its melody of afflictions.

The brief seconds she stands alone in darkness and silence feel warped and painfully extended. "I was hiding in your shadow the whole time," he says from behind her. Cassidy's stomach drops in dread. "What is going on? How can I fight this differently?" she thinks to herself, "Well I have to keep going. I'm a hero now, for many," she continues to say as she reminds herself of the look on peoples faces when she saved them. This lights her up inside fueling her for the next round of this obscure battle. "I have to be a warrior for others. This is far more than just for myself. It is my love that gives me light and strength that has always instilled fear in you," she says aloud to the Illusionist in the pitch black dark, "When exactly did you die inside Raziel and why?" The Illusionist doesn't respond yet these words fill him with subtle torment and provoking indignation. Without responding he initiates the first attack in the darkness. With her sense of worth to the world she fights harder and more able than before. Without the visual illusion

Cassidy is able to attack back more efficiently with the raw sense of her spirit.

It is not long before she feels something else isn't right. A sensation of tension wraps around her neck and she is pulled up high into the air by her neck. The fight stops and the candle flames light up once again. After the sensation of being pulled up into the air she is yet also able to look up at herself from the floor. With herself split into two she sees herself being hung by a rope mid air and struggling looking down yet she also stands in front of him at the same time. "Which one is the real me?" she contemplates in outstanding fear as she knows and feels her soul in both places. Her only response to end this torment is to simply conquer the battle now. Cassidy is able to grab ahold of the Illusionist's suit and out of rage and supernatural strength launches him over her hip slamming him on the hard floor. She drags him back up and the grappling continues. Throw after throw continues until she is able to implement the most enthralling toss slamming and pinning the Illusionist on the floor. She lay on top of him with her face next to his. "Why Raziel?" she asks. His face then begins to melt and distort onto the floor until he remain completely liquid on the ground into a puddle of paint. Cassidy looks up at her other self suffering hanging above her. She flies up to herself and breaks her other self free bringing herself softly to the ground. Once landing back on the ground her other self fades away in her arms. The liquid puddle of the Illusionist begins to disappear like the last bit of water vaporizing on a hot pan.

THE CHILD'S CRY

A small door opens in the room and Cassidy hesitates to follow the obvious lead but knows there is no where else to go and this has to end soon for all moments end. The door is only about three to four feet high and children's laughter comes from behind the inviting opening. The small door creaks as she gradually opens it more. Peering inside she sees a dirt tunnel filled with roots and vines leading to a place that emanates the feeling of joyous memories of childhood and exuding joyful classical music. Drawn by the temptation of the peace she feels coming from the other side she follows through the tunnel reaching for the distant peace. Arriving to the other side of the tunnel light permeates through the cracks in another door and without hesitation she opens it to see an exquisite room full of merry and pleasant looking people with all appearing from the victorian era.

Music plays and people cheer in laughter and conversation like a reunion of friends. Cassidy steps inside hypnotized and unaware she is being trapped by the illusion of her deep desire of benevolence. She smiles and absorbs the comforting sensation in the air forgetting about everything. People dance and enjoy themselves and Cassidy begins to partake in the party. Hours pass of pleasure and she heads toward the fireplace to rest. Out of the corner of her eye she notices one of the cordial men with a white peruke wig appearing with the face of the Illusionist. Cassidy freezes in the middle of the room as reality stirs back to her like an unwinding vortex. She begins to look all around her now noticing everyone in the room has the face of the Illusionist. All the men and all the women, they are all him. All people in the room one after another turn around to face her. With the hypnotizing spell unraveling in her mind she now stands in the middle of the room surrounded as they begin to laugh hideously at her. Cassidy collapses to her knees hiding her face in her hands on the floor for she can take no more mental torment.

Crying in her hands she feels pity for herself, "I thought I was stronger. I thought I was better," she says to herself, "I now understand more than ever being a great warrior means to also be just as strong in the mind as well. How did I let it get this far with him. I have fallen for every trap." Cassidy continues to cry as laughter at her continues as well. She digs deep into her mind, "Stop letting him lead you into his trap. You have the knowledge and power to absorb his skills and use it against him. What does his soul fear? What will crack his own stability?" Cassidy then figures it out. She know much of his story and his past. Not all of it but enough.

As she continues to cry on the floor she for the first time is able to use the magic of transmutation. The gift the Magician only gave to Raziel and she then embodies the child of the Illusionist Raziel. As she transmutes and becomes the child Raziel once was now crying helplessly on the floor the laughter begins to fade away. The laughter trickles away until it is silent. Cassidy continues to weep as the child of Raziel. She looks up around the room as him to see all the faces of the Illusionist looking at her in despair as she weeps. He feels the pain he had forgotten so long ago of the child he was that is now before him. It is something he wants to keep buried forever. Continuing with her ability she transmutes the room now into the streets of his childhood. Homeless and without, isolated and cold she creates and embodies it all to perfection. "No more of you only creating Raziel. Fear who I am becoming," she says inside to herself in confidence. His multiple forms walk over to whom he sees as the child of him with compassion. All his forms begin to weep as well around the child closely reaching for him.

One of his forms comes to the child and embraces him. He holds the child and they both cry together. "I am sorry little Raziel! I am so sorry!" the Illusionist cries and continues to break down like an infant. Tears flood the ground which appears as his homeless streets and the other illusions of himself begin to dissipate. He doesn't mind that it all crumbles away for he cradles the child of him and his former innocence. They both howl in grievance, so much so that the Illusionist cannot mentally keep tact of the carnival illusion anymore. Everything begins to fade and the Illusionist is now in the middle of the desert holding the child. Touching the deepest parts of his hidden pains he doesn't mind or care and yet he cannot let go of cradling the child. "I am so sorry," he whispers to the child of himself as he kisses the forehead of the child.

Once he kisses the child peace floods the atmosphere and he opens his eyes to the quiet empty desert. He looks into his arms and the child is no longer there yet Cassidy being held looks back into his suffering eyes. Too broken to fight he realizes he is the one whom is defeated. The Illusionist stands up and continues to look at her with his swollen eyes and at the sun ready to emerge over the horizon. "What happened to you Cassidy? Whom have you become?" asks the Illusionist. "I chose to obey the light," she replies and stands up, "Some think if you go to the darkness there is no resurrection of your soul yet I can testify." The Illusionist unable to digest the words she speaks can only turn away and walk in the defeat of inward eyes to his own soul. "I don't stand here to condemn you. I am here to give you a new beginning," Cassidy says. The Illusionist hears what Cassidy says but continues onward in the dark desert toward the now rising sun on the horizon.

CHAPTER 10

WALTZ OF THE ETERNAL FLOWER

Cassidy heads into her abode to rest from the exhaustion of the all night battle between her and the Illusionist that felt like days. Her feeling of victory is a gradual and delayed response as there is much to digest of her mental overcomings. Some of the horrific images of the battle run repeatedly through her mind as she falls deep asleep. The night had surfaced many deep rooted strongholds on her character and she knows there is more to aspire in her mental and spiritual strength. However it be, she conquered many of her own fears in the illusions that transpired in the fight and obtained the forbidden gift of illusion to herself. A gift thought only to be bestowed by the Magician.

Upon awakening Cassidy feels a surge of fuel through her like an amplitude of vitality. The sun is close to setting already for she has slept through the day. She remembers tonight is the evening of the ball at Mr. White's mansion. A foreign sensation of butterflies in her heart surprises her. Something she hadn't felt and forgotten about since she was a young girl performing and fell in love for the first time. "Am I really nervous for a dance?" she asks out loud to herself. Feeling a little weak she sighs, "Oh dear, looks like I might just be." She laughs loudly and smiles as she heads over to her old record player, lifts the needle and sets it back down ready to play melodies of old. The crackling sound of the music beginning brings her comfort and Cassidy heads downstairs to get ready a bath that looks like an old glorified wooden barrel. She pours in water heated from the stove and swirls her hand through the water before entering. She pulls off her clothes throwing them onto the nearby chair and sinks her alluring physique into the comforting water. Leaning her head back she says, "Now that I know how people bath these days maybe I should get myself set up a lil' better around this ol' joint." Cassidy then submerges into the water completely letting her enthusiasm stew in the heated waters.

At Mr. White's mansion lights are fancied around the entry gate and early arrivals of friends begin to show up in the most exquisite of vehicles. The sound of musicians beginning to warm up their various instruments paints the air with bliss. White makes his way over to the conductor to ask him, "What scores do you have prepared to play during the last hours of the night?" "Was there something particular you were looking for sir?" the conductor asks him politely. "Actually yes, there is in fact. I have someone very special arriving whom has saved my life more than once. When she arrives near the ballroom floor begin to play Tchaikovsky's Walts of the Flowers please," Mr. White replies. The conductor agrees in gesture and asks him, "How will I know it is her?" "Because everyone will turn heads at her gracious appearance," responds Mr. White in the most confident tone. "Also apologies for my curiosity but why that particular score for this mysterious woman?" the conductor asks. "For the beauty of this flower never fades nor does its aroma cease to leave enchantment," replies Mr. White. "Enough said sir, and I shall play it better than I ever have before. What a splendid night this will be!" the conductor says with amusement and a quick wink of his eye.

Within hours the mansion is full of exquisite gowns and tailored gentlemen. The evening exudes a whimsical and playful fantasy captivating minds with memories to cherish. Noble men and women elegantly waltz across the grand marble floor. Fine wine and hors d'oeuvre is served throughout while everyone is captivated by the joys this night holds.

Cassidy arrives at the front gates and she hears the jubilant laughter and delightful music. She walks proudly forward looking stunning and regal through the long walkway toward the entry door stairs hearing Strauss's, "Voices of Spring Waltz." Cassidy confidently continues up to the front door feeling and looking more beautiful than ever before. Two gentlemen graciously open the large doors for her to enter. As she steps into the foyer she sees herself in a grand and gold decorated mirror. She is taken aback at how she looks tonight through the full length mirror for she has never felt like a princess but tonight she can see for herself she is far more than even that. While gazing into the mirror the grandfather clock behind her in the foyer strikes the tune of eleven thirty. Holding her head high she opens the doors to the ballroom and becomes completely hypnotized by the charm.

Standing in the ballroom door entryway people one by one begin rippling like a tide to turn their heads to look at her notable appearance for she is gorgeous yet abstract amongst the normal colors of the room. The sea of mortals part as she gazes toward White's direction. Mr. White far across the other side of the room turns around through the parting to see Cassidy in such elegance and eminence he pauses in reverence. His breath is taken away as his eyes dive deep into her spirit. Her seductive and enchanting eyes rest like dark jewels on her polished face. A delicate black and golden crown compliments her face and pierces downward in direction with her sharp windows peak while gold and diamonds of antiquity and rarity adorn her neck delicately. The bodice of the gown is shaped to that of a ballerina. It is made of black satin and embellished as well with diamonds and gold. The dress leads down to sheer black fabric dropping down to her feet yet with the front shorter showing her stunning legs and adorned feet.

Noticing her obvious arrival the conductor in mid Strauss stops his musicians to begin the, "Waltz of the Flowers," as requested. The score begins and White's eyes are locked and spellbound into Raven's darkly painted seductive eyes. The harp begins its soliloquy as she graces across the room to him through the parting and all seem to stand still. White gestures to hold her hand to accept a dance and he bows his head and kisses her hand placed gently in his white glove. "May I have this dance with you Raven?" he asks her. She nods her head in agreement and holds her gown with her left hand to curtsy. The waltz begins and Mr. White holds Raven's lower back with one hand and the other hand to hand. He leads her across the ballroom circling the perimeter floating and in bewilderment they dance. Magnetized into her eyes he says to her, "You look more beautiful than there are words for." Looking back into his eyes her heart softens more and touching the woman in her that was never able to blossom in the world. "Thank you for inviting me," Raven says. He spins her in and leaning her back he holds her in his arms to say, "It is my greatest pleasure Raven." Their faces are close enough to feel the heat of each others breath and smell the faint scent of each others dispositions. Spellbound into her eyes and beauty he pulls her back to him and continues to dance across the room with the black silken fabric trailing behind them like a live fluid painting.

The waltz begins to come to a closure and as the intensity of the ending score builds they spiral around quicker entertaining each other. The music ends and before the next score plays Mr. White says to her, "I have something very special for you." Raven looks at him with confusion. "Yes, I was told so. What is it?" she asks. "It was left for me to give to you from Slinger. He made sure to mention how important it was for it to be in your hands and your hands only," he replies. "Well let me see it!" Raven hastily says. Mr. White looks around the room knowing most will wonder where they disappeared to. He sighs to himself knowing most will talk and make suspicions anyway. "Okay then. Come with me," he says as he leads her out of the ballroom holding her hand and upstairs to his room.

DEEP WATERS WASH ASHORE

Entering the room they stand in modest awkwardness. "The last time I was in this room I tried to kill you," she says. "Yes I remember. How could I forget," he replies, "Raven the way you look tonight you have surely taken part of my breath and my soul, but even since the first time I saw you I adored you. Even though you wanted to kill me you still captured my heart." He pulls her in close to his body, "I love you Raven," he says as his lips touch hers and they embraces in a kiss with one foot in the water. Then their heart beats begin to synchronize like the beat of a tribal war drum and heat elates through their core with every subsequent kiss. He collapses into her defenseless to her spellbinding allure. Exposed of her heart she falls weak from his kisses and throws her head back as he begins to plunge into her breasts. They crash back onto the bed and fall hostage to the carnal desires. A tsunami of passion floods them and they carelessly become casualties of love.

The mirror across the room over looking the bed reflects moonlight onto Raven making her bare skin luminous. He drives into her body and they sing in release over the orchestral symphony downstairs. Any heaviness of consequences is absent for they are absolved of their succumbing and exonerated in self defense. The decorated mirror watches them with the burning eyes of the Magician. As they spiral deeper into the ignited passion the Magician's fury sends blazing fire into the mirror yet they are too far submerged under water and unable to notice anything but each other. The night continues and hours pass with tears of fire trickling down the Magician's face. He continues to watch ensnared with agony and rage. As the passings of the night come to a closure and the symphony ends, the melody of waltzes and intertwining of flesh continues repetitively in the Magician's mind.

The storm has settled and Raven and Mr. White lay washed ashore on white sheets and the clock sounds of three a.m. She lays on her stomach propped up on her elbows and her bare body is that of a sculpture. She asks Mr. White, "What was it you wanted to give me?" "Oh yes, let me get it," Mr. White says as he gets up out of bed and goes to his locked safe in his closet. He enters a code and grabs the items from Slinger. He heads back to Raven and places them in front of her. Raven knowing these are extremely important items she sits up and props back on her knees with her long hair cascading over her chest. First she looks at the mysterious black book with the numbers inscribed, "2222." "I could not open it," says White. Raven then gradually opens the old book and sees a box made of yew wood hidden inside. She delicately places her hand over the box and opens it with ease. Inside she sees an odd object wrapped in very old white linen. Unraveling the cloth a magnificent golden key falls into her hands.

All falls silent within her for she is awestruck by the beauty and sensation the key holds. She can tell it is of pure gold and that it resonates a dignified and superior power. It feels celestial in her hands and she wraps it back into the white linen and places it back into the box. She closes the wooden box immediately. Raven then opens the hand sized purple bag unraveling the drawstrings and pulls out a stunning, embellished silver key. She admires the beauty and feels the wisdom within this key and places it back into the purple bag. Raven then grabs the envelope sealed with red wax. Opening the envelope slowly and carefully she then pulls out a letter written by Slinger. "Cassidy, I'm sure you opened the box first and are now reading this letter. The golden key within that box is destined for you and you only. You will be able to open and close what no one else can. You will know when the time is right and what it is for. Make sure that the keys I gave you will not be in anyone else's hands! The silver key opens the door to a secret library where you can access the most ancient knowledge and wisdom of this world and the forbidden knowledge and forbidden wisdom of the otherworld. You will find it on, 'Elysium Road.' Enter through the back and the door will say, 'Library of Nemeton.' Stay steadfast in your righteousness and all that will follow is greatness. Bring light to the world and abolish fears. I always loved you like a daughter Cassidy. Thank you for being in my life. Goodbye."

Raven's heart sinks into her belly as she knows the reason Slinger gave such important items to her. She senses that he knows it is inevitable that he will be captured back into the Magician's terrifying captivity and subject to the chains of eternal suffering. "What is it? What's wrong?" White asks her concerned. "Nothing... Actually just a lot to digest... Well Slinger is in undeniable trouble and I feel there is nothing I can do," replies Raven knowing White wouldn't be able to fathom what she knows. "You're a superhero are you kidding me?" he says running his hand down her bare back. "Well one thing is for sure, the final battle is inescapable for me. I must face the master who breeds darkness throughout this world," Raven says. "Are you sure you can defeat darkness itself?" White says taken aback. "Defeat no, subdue yes," Raven replies and then gets up to put her gown back on. "You are leaving? Stay with me," White says. "There is too much, just way too many very pivotal events unfolding. I have to leave now," she says continuing to get dressed. "Is that statue of the giant going to be there forever?" asks White peering out the window seeing the screaming frozen Abatu looking through the window back at him. "I'll see what I can do," Raven smiles. Mr. White stands up and gives her a warming kiss and says, "You have brought me so much happiness back into my life Raven." He then runs his fingers through her long hair and kisses her again on her forehead.

Raven exits the mansion and heads down the stairs. She pauses to look at Abatu frozen in stone to her right along the path and she contemplates the day she cast him into that form. She feels compassion for Abatu for she knew his former self before the influences of the Magician. Raven goes to place her right hand on the stone statue of the giant Abatu. Her hand touches the cold stone and she says to him, "Abatu, when your heart begins to soften the stone will begin to break. However long it need be is up to you, but I do miss you friend and this is all that can break the spell."

CHAPTER 11

FATE OF BETRAYAL

Slinger wanders around the city never resting too long in any one place. His nerves are building and he knows confrontation is coming soon. He momentarily finds brief refuge and rests inside an old bar in a broken part of town. Finally as he becomes the last man in the bar the exhausted bartender says to him, "Come on now, time to go. It's late and we're closing our doors." Slinger then looks down into his glass of whisky and says sadly, "But my drink is still full." The bartender cleaning the counter leans forward with a cheerless face and replies, "Sometimes we have to leave before we're finished." Slinger doesn't say anything and gets up to leave knowing the time has come. Turning around he sees through the windows dark shadows quickly passing by outside seeming to taunt him. He knows he has no choice but to go out there and he hopes in wishful thinking to find another place of refuge right away. Slinger also knows he cannot rest at Cassidy's home for he wouldn't want to bring her anymore trouble than what she has to face on her own.

Slinger steps outside and feels the cold dark forbidding wind. The city is silent and restlessness builds in the air. He looks at his bike parked down the street and it seems too far to make it yet it is so close. Again he has no choice. He walks slowly down the street toward his bike and with each step he hears his boots hit the brisk pavement. He hears his warm breath hit the raw and cold air as it forms a resistance of fog. Almost there now he has to cross a dark alley before reaching his bike. He avoids with his eyes the darkness to the left in the alley as he begins to cross in fearful denial of what lays in the shadows. Before he makes it across a cold hand yanks and drags him deep into the alley.

Slinger hesitantly opens his eyes to see three dark forms in front of him. He knows what the are. They are trapped soul slaves of the Magician who have transmuted into demons. Within an instant of his recognition of who they are all three race toward him with a ghastly scream. Slinger pulls out his pistols and fires away with supernatural precision as always. It only sets them back temporarily and they continue to progress at him. He continues to fire at an astonishing speed spinning and twirling the guns around him. The multidimensional beings can't be stopped by mere bullets however his accuracy and speed keeps them struggling as he tries to escape the alley heading to the light at the opening. Eventually the beings bombard him as he almost reaches the light. In the brief second of a possibility of victory Slinger finds himself paralyzed as they all grab ahold of his being. He has to surrender as a motionless corpse yet with his eyes still filled with his spirit.

Out of the far back in the alley and in total darkness Slinger hears the sinister and familiar chuckles of the Magician.

Smoke trails out of the darkness and out steps the Magician in the mist of his smoke. "Did you really think you could escape me? You have been on the run for so long Slinger what did you think was going to magically happen for you? Did you think Cassidy was going to save you? She isn't strong enough to defeat me," he says strolling forward toward Slinger, "So it is Raven they call her now. A hero? She will see that she is no hero and neither are you. You're both servants to me and belong to me for eternity for I bestowed my gifts and immortality unto you both. I will crush her like a small bird in my hand," he continues to say as he clenches his fist over his heart, "And you! You know where you are headed with me now. For no soul shall betray and escape damnation."

Slinger still stands paralyzed with the three demons holding him. All he can do is listen to the Magician's words and feel the nauseating pain of true fear. Even at this point he does not regret the decisions he made thus far for he made a promise to himself for this moment so long ago. The Magician walks past Slinger and signals the beings to take him along home. As the Magician passes Slinger's bike he decides to take it for himself and ride it home. He blasts off on Slingers beloved bike and the grim beings fly Slinger home to the Magician's mansion.

THE APPETITE OF THE BOTTOMLESS PIT

While still paralyzed and incapable of moving Slinger is flown down the cold stone stairs deep into the chambers of the Magician's underworld. The Magician casually walks and follows behind as they transport him through the chambers. As they pass the many closed doors stillness and sorrow floods the many mysterious characters behind the walls for all cringe at knowing what will befall. Slinger is carried toward the furthest vault down through the last hall of the chambers. Inside he tries to mentally prepare himself for what is to come. Anxiety builds behind his frozen body as they all head deeper into the most dreaded corner of the world.

Arriving at the final and last door Slinger still tries to scream yet you can only hear it through his eyes. The Illusionist stands waiting at the door for the Magician as he is aways ready and by his side. The door is surrounded by carved stone filled with faces of despair, pain, regret, and guilt. Some faces are large and some of them small yet all are intertwined. The door is the deepest of reds and of such aged wood it is petrified stone. There is no handle on this door and only one can open this door with mere words. The Magician proudly recites his words of magic, "NEGELTU ASAR ETUTU! 'Awake Eye of Darkness.'" All pause and the door opens slightly from the left. The Magician's hand pushes it completely open and they all step through. The door slams behind them and they all wait in the total and complete dark with an undeniable feeling of being watched, observed, and judged.

Raziel the Illusionist lights a candle for the Magician to find his way to the middle of the room. A petrified wooden table lay in the middle of the room awaiting them. It is simple and has only a small hole in the middle of the table. Beneath the hole of the table is a hole in the floor and funnel like in shape. The Magician's three spirits lay Slinger atop the table and tears falls from his frozen face. The Illusionist drops his head unable to see Slinger here like this in such agony for when the eyes can talk words become unnecessary. The Magician has never seen Raziel show empathy, not at least since he was a child. The Magician notices this and turns his head toward the Illusionist waiting for him to make eye contact. Raziel lifts his head back up finally to see the Magician staring into him making a point of noticing his altered consciousness.

The table begins to tremble and there is a sense of impatience in the heavy air. The Magician speaks grave and solemn, "Slinger, what a journey we have had and how well you have served me, however nothing can take away the punishment of betrayal. For this you and your eternal soul and flesh shall lay in suffering, bleeding for eternity feeding the darkness. As your eternal being slowly loses your sense of self completely you will be consumed by the darkness and forgotten forever." The Magician then takes out from the base of the table a long, thin, and narrow silver blade. He feels the blade through his gloved fingers taking his time to observe it. He places it over Slinger and slowly pushes it through his flesh penetrating his abdomen all the way reaching the hole in the table. The Magician then slowly pulls the blade out and blood trickles drop by drop into the hole in the ground. Slinger makes eye contact with the Illusionist one last time. Slinger can sense something has changed in Raziel. His last hope of possibly ever being saved would only be through compassion. They all begin to depart the uncomfortable room leaving Slinger behind frozen on the table.

The door opens back up for them once they get close to it and they exit. Once the door closes behind them the Magician releases his spirits. "WASSURU GENII WARDUM, 'Release the spirit slaves,'" he says and loudly claps his hands as the souls vanish away. The Magician and the Illusionist begin to walk together back down the hall. It is awkward for the Illusionist as the Magician knows he failed at his last attack at Raven yet he hasn't mentioned why. "How did you fail your mission Raziel? How did she defeat you?" Samael asks. "My lord, my apologies," Raziel replies dropping his head, "I was conquering until the very end. I thought she fell into my last trap for she was surely falling apart yet it was her in the end that trapped me. Who she is becoming is a great force spiraling larger everyday." The Magician continues to walk and look expressionlessly straight forward digesting what he hears. They finally reach the end of the chambers and stand at the bottom of the stairs to head back up to the world. "Raven has yet to face me and she will most definitely arrive once she feels the sorrows coming from Slinger's cries of his soul," the Magician says. The Illusionist takes one left step onto the first stair and pauses to ask the Magician a question he has always wanted to ask him, "Lord, why do you never fight your own battles?" The Magician looks at him and replies, "The wise man never uses his own hands in battle for victory. Yet he uses his mind to manipulate others to play out his deck of cards masterfully." The Illusionist and the Magician then head up the stairs and exit the chambers.

CHAPTER 12

ARMY OF DARKNESS

Cassidy rests at her home and lays back into her bath looking across the room at her gown thrown on the floor daydreaming and pondering the evening before. She gets out of the bath and puts on one of her old fashioned all white linen nightgowns. It is simple and pure in design. Cassidy then walks over into the kitchen and sits down at her old wooden kitchen table. The evening sun comes through the kitchen window and gently caresses her face. She has a slight sensation of hunger and looks down at the flat bread on the table in front of her. On the table are also the sacred items that were recently bestowed to her. The black book with the golden key, the purple sachet with the silver key, and the sealed note written from Slinger. She begins to daydream to herself momentarily how kind and lovely Mr. White was to her. She reminisces on how beautiful she felt in her dress dancing across the ballroom floor. Cassidy can sense inside this is a moment to behold for this is her last resting breath before the battle of dualities. She breaks the bread in half and consumes some from the right while still enjoying the warm sun on her face. She then also grabs the bread broken onto the left side of her. As she begins to eat more of this bread she gets a sickening feeling in her belly. Something isn't right. At his moment Cassidy knows it is Slinger. He is captive and she can feel the cries of his soul. Unable to rest any longer Cassidy knows surely tonight is the night. She stands up from the table and the sunlight now sets beyond the horizon. With a fierce determination she readies herself for battle.

Cassidy begins to suit up in her attire and amour while the sound of ravens swam restlessly outside her abode. Tensions build on the earthly plane for the unseen forces have already commenced in utter war. The girl she once was is now called Raven a warrior who flies in the seam of the mysterious veil between light and dark. More ready and confident than ever before she heads steadfast with a white hot fire fueling her every cell and quenching her ravishing soul. She heads outside into the streets of her lonely western town. Standing in the middle of the dirt road all alone Raven spins slowly around and the ravens above still swarm as a legion above her. She absorbs the moment of how far she has come. So much she has overcome and conquered. She finally takes the time to appreciate the hero she has become. The friends she had and the ones she lost. All that pushed her to her greatest good and all that stood against her. She loves every part of her journey and now graciously accepts and enjoys her immortality.

Looking up into the beautiful night sky she launches herself into the air high above the town twirling like a vortex. At the peak of her momentum into the sky she explosively expands her large wings and her whole body becomes illuminated in the night sky. Tonight there is no moon in the sky to give her light yet it is her own being that now radiates from within. She looks down onto the town and reminisces the day the Magician cast his spell and all the destruction, pain, and suffering he caused. Raven thinks about it all and how he will finally be subdued tonight. Knowing she doesn't have an exact plan, the burning desire to conquer is sufficient enough. She flies off out of the town heading to the inner city with a fever to triumph.

The Magician feels Raven's arrival is soon and needs more time. He knows tonight is the battle of gods. He steps up onto an altar in his bedroom and calls upon his league of the dead. "WASSURU UMMANATE MITUTU!" he says, "Release my army of dead." He then places his hands upon an embellished box fully decorated in rare gems and gold. He breathes out his mysterious smoke from his mouth and it sinuously slides into the lock that holds it carefully closed. The smoke unlocks the small extravagant box only cracking it open slightly. A stentorian voice comes from deep within the box asking, "For you who have unlocked us what is your calling for us master?" The Magician then replies to the mysterious voice, "Capture Raven and seize her. Bring her to me and destroy all that comes within you path." The voice in the box then remains with an empty momentary pause. "Your command is granted," the voice replies and the box is flung open immediately and a purge of souls flee out from the box rapidly swarming through the halls of the mansion and out the front door. They flood the streets screaming hideously on their way to their mission heading toward the city.

Raven soars through the night sky swiftly toward the Magician with urgency. As she arrives close to the inner city she can hear the horrible cries of the many spirits flooding her way. She picks up speed to arrive in time for she knows what they are and what tyranny they are capable of. Raven knows the Magician sensed her arrival and released them to set her back with damaging chaos yet she fearlessly heads quicker towards them. The city is unusually quite for a Saturday evening. The few left out scurry amongst the streets into hiding like animals with an intuition of a catastrophe. Raven sees ahead the tall golden casino and aims for her landing. She angles herself and her wings to land from such force and speed. As she touches down atop the building she kneels down perched over the edge peering down into the streets below with her wings still extended looking statuesque and heroic. The army of spirits is but a minute away now and their chilling cries are becoming unbearable and the earth trembles in forewarning. Raven stands up tall now seeing the spirits flooding the streets like a tsunami from just a couple miles away. Raven then jumps down from atop the building landing in the middle of the empty city street facing the flood. She lets her wings fade back and she draws from her back her favorite and beloved double swords. Now a lone warrior standing with a blade in each hand she awaits the few seconds that are left before the Magician's army of darkness.

ONE HUNDRED FORTY FOUR THOUSAND

Like the breath before a collision all one hundred and forty four thousand soldiers are yet yards away from Raven's face. They are screaming with their mouths open ready to annihilate anything in their path. Raven charges forward just as fearless toward them sprinting ahead with blades ready to obliterate them all as she screams right back at them. Raven charges straight through the dark spirits decimating anything coming close to her. Her blade work is that of magic and skill and she is the dancing warrior destroying all that comes in her path against her. There are only sounds of rapidly sliced flesh and the screams of demons against one warrior of light. Hours pass as Raven continues through the furious demons in flesh massacring his army.

Raven continues with fire and might but eventually begins to get bombarded in the heaviest and most condensed part of the swarm. She launches herself up out of the battlefield into mid air to avoiding being consumed. She looks down as the swarm begins to follow up towards her creating stairs in thin air as they voraciously climb atop one another to her. Lifting her blades high above her head she waits till many follow pursuit and she then jolts herself spiraling down eradicating all beneath her propelling her blades downward with her supernatural force.

Raven lands back on the ground again witnessing only a fraction of the army left around her. She stands surrounded by rotten demon flesh and the last standing soldiers of darkness. With them too scattered at this point Raven begins to ponder her next method of attack. In that moment three of the largest of the demons begin to march straight toward her. They seem different than the rest with more power and intelligence than the others. Raven slashes at the two in front of her setting their attacks back. Right when she is about to eliminate the two with her left sword across their necks the third huge demon spirit from behind her knocks out of her right hand her beloved sword. Raven becomes beyond enraged as she watches the sword fall far across the concrete for her swords are sacred and precious to her almost more than anything. She turns around to face the demon as he begins to laugh at her, mocking and gloating in an opportunity to dim her bright spirit. They all see this as their golden opportunity to destroy Raven with one sword down.

Raven quickly grabs her chain out of her setup and immediately begins to spin her weapon at unimaginable speed around her keeping all that is left at bay. The chain is then swung swiftly around the mocking demon's neck and his laughter ceases as she pulls him in swiftly with the chain to defeat him with ease slashing him with her left sword. Raven continues with this tactic one by one wrapping and catching the chain around the necks with the right and slashing with the left. All until the very last one stands before her, number one hundred forty four thousand. She walks over to him as she puts her chain away. The demon hisses and snarls at her as she gets closer. Raven stands a foot away from his face to feel the fear now coming from the darkness within this creature and she momentarily pities for him.

"You may destroy us all now but our master will resurrect us again," the last demon cries with laughter. "Know for that the one hundred and forty four thousand there is of darkness there is the one hundred and forty four thousand of the light," Raven replies. She stands curiously only to look deep into his dark eyes and can not feel anything in them but a void and thus feels sorrow for the darkness. An energy that can only consume what is good and only knows how to do just that. Raven then slashes the very last standing demon before her across his neck and he collapses to the concrete laughing until his very last breath as he whispers to her, "Raven! Do you really know who you are?" Raven looks into his eyes as they dissolve away and ponders what he said knowing this moment will surely resurface in her mind forever. She then looks around at all that lay before her and absorbs her moment of victory from a place of duty and service to not only her own soul but her destiny. All the soldiers of darkness that lay scattered in the streets of the urban battlefield begin to dissipate into the air like particulate matter. The sounds of their screams spiral into an invisible warp until the sound itself is collapsed into nothingness.

Raven then sees her beloved right sword before her and goes to pick it up. She ever so slightly smiles as she puts her blades behind her back and continues down the empty street. Launching back up into the air she heads steadfast yet again to her final destiny at the Magician's lair.

CHAPTER 13

IT IS WRITTEN

Raven arrives out front of the Magician's prodigal mansion at the end of the long walkway beholding what awaits her. She lands on her feet and stands with her wings spread triumphantly. The Magician sits in his throne in the back of his mansion. He senses her arrival and can see her with his inner eye standing out front. Out of spite and jealousy of her joyous dance with Mr. White he begins to pervade the air with a symphony. "Well Cassidy if it's a waltz you want and enjoy my child then let us dance!" he says aloud to himself as the loud symphony permeates the space yet coming from no source. She knows it is time and steps forward with her left foot and continues cautiously one foot at a time heading toward the dark mansion.

Once arriving at the front doors that stand well over twelve feet tall and embroidered with esoteric designs sense her advent and they graciously open on their own for her homecoming. Raven begins to strongly sense Slinger's suffering and is more enraged than ever with the Magician. "His madness must come to an end tonight and peace shall prevail," she says inside to herself as she steps through the doorway. Now inside and standing with pride and indignation in his lair she reminisces on all the suffering and agony he caused her and others. In a courageous outburst Raven shouts calling his name aloud, "Samael!" she shouts forcing herself forward. "Samaeeeeeeel!" she shouts again continuing forward, "I am here for you Samael! Show yourself unto me!" she screams as it echoes over and over throughout the empty halls.

Once the echoing finally comes to an end and trickles off in its last words the Magician replies to her, "If you like to dance Raven then come over here and dance with me!" Raven then charges forward toward his voice through the long halls sprinting all the way finding the very back of the building. She sees the final and last doors ahead of her and does not hesitate to continue nor does any fear make way. She bursts through his bedroom doors without qualm and they slam shut behind her. It is a large room and he sits in his throne all the way in the back across the room yet in front of her. Off across to the right of the room is his lavish bed and to the left of the room is his altar. She steps further into the room and heaviness bombards the air. "Where is Slinger?" she shouts to him. "No need for you to worry about him for it is already sealed. He is far beneath us in the last vault in the chambers below. A door you cannot open," the Magician calmly replies, "What brings you here Raven? I see you made it I am not surprised." "I incinerated your army," Raven replies. "For now, that is. They can be summoned again Cassidy. Don't you think I would know out of all people you have what it takes to defeat an army? Don't you remember the hand who fed you and taught you such skills?" the Magician says to her. Raven then pulls out her swords and holds them tightly by the side of her tense body. The Magician carelessly flicks his finger and her swords are flown back against the wall behind her like the pulling force of a magnet. Proceeding her swords all of her weapons are stripped and forced out of her setup and drawn against the wall except for the hidden copper dagger.

Raven's confidence drops as she is stripped of her weapons. She knows his skill of magic and mental battle surpass hers. "Let's just talk Raven. Maybe we can sort this mess out you know." Raven feels a supernatural force urging and drawing her to walk toward him as the air thickens and heaviness drenches her. He stands up out of his throne and walks over to meet her as well. With Raven now in the middle of the room and almost incapable of moving the Magician collides in front of her and runs his hands through her beautiful hair down over her breast and over her belly. "Raven you know I love you and you haven't yet seen that it is my love that you seek," he whispers to her on her neck. "Come to me child," he says pulling her in close and she helpless falls into the deepest hole of the unbearable spell of desire. A thin mist of smoke fills the atmosphere and he engages his lips against hers. Cassidy falls limp in his embracing arms and he carries her to his lavish bed of red silk. A rage of lust fills them both as he strips her of her clothes and his lips caress every corner of her flesh. He manipulates her body filling her with a hunger unable to content desperately reaching for more.

The Magician thrusts into her and they become one in this sacred moment. Cassidy screams with unbearable pleasure for this is his moment to subdue her. She falls deeper and deeper into this lustful paradise outside the capsule of time.

Only a dwindling fraction of her conscious remains and she desperately tries to not let go of the last bit she has. He rolls onto his back to see her beauty above him and she unchains herself from guilt of the carnality. A coiling serpentine wave of energy deluges up throughout her being as she reaches a pinnacle of unfathomable pleasure. He reaches for the moment he has waited for to release his sprit and air unto her. Still trying to hold on to her last percent of her conscious Raven sees his pinnacle of liberation as she is unto the same. She uses every bit of will she has and grabs out of her clothes beside her the copper dagger she took from him. As they both reach their final release together she thrusts down onto his heart the sacred copper dagger.

His eyes look into hers with an unfathomable look of betrayal. He screams in pain and agony as his last waves of pleasure roll through her body. "Cassidy why? Why Cassidy!" he cries looking down at the dagger and his love seated atop of him. "Why do I hurt so badly? I... I never feel pain! This can't be true!" He looks back into her with eyes of tribulation and a fractured heart.

KISS THE WOUNDED DRAGON

Raven gets off the bed as the spell of lust begins to subside. She grabs a cigar out of his clothes and makes her way over to his throne. Raven sits down naked into his throne claiming it as hers and lights his cigar. She breathes in power and exhales victory. The Magician lays weak on the bed unable to comprehend what he is truly feeling as he bleeds from his shattered heart and gazes into her beautiful eyes. "Cassidy... Cassidy! What have you done!" he cries. She gently looks back at him from the throne seeing him so weakened and powerless now. While resting her head back onto the throne she knows the war isn't quite yet complete. "I did what I had to do. It was written. I am sorry it had to be," she peacefully replies. "Why did you cause me so much pain? Why so much suffering and isolation?" she asks him.

The Magician begins to try and stand off the bed yet he falls to the ground with a thud and gasping for air. The Magician continues to struggle but only makes his way to his hands and knees and says to her, "All I ever wanted was a real love. No one can fathom the pain I experience of complete rejection of any light since the beginning of time. I am more alone than you have ever felt Cassidy. I thought if I brought you to a similar place of pain you could love me and we could share that forever." Cassidy leans forward from his throne. "You destroyed everything I loved. I was not deserving of what you afflicted unto me. Did you think murdering all I cared for would really make me love you?" she says to him. The Magician crawls across the floor to her sitting in his throne with a trail of his blood now at her feet. "If I let you stay with your lover and if I didn't murder him... You would have faded away with a simple life and you would've been nobody and forgotten to everyone forever. I loved you too much. I gave you your new everlasting life Cassidy. Without the loss, isolation, humiliation, the sacrifice, and the breaking of your spirit you would not have birthed into the legend of Raven you are now," he says and props himself up on one knee beneath her now and slowly begins to try and stand in her presence. Cassidy stands up from the chair and she helps lift his weak body up to her. "Don't you see why I am necessary Cassidy? My darkness has a place in this world. Without me your light would have never emerged to shine so bright," he says as he now crawls himself all the way up to her still bleeding profusely from his heart. He leans in to kiss her lips and she without any spell kisses him back for she has found a small place of love within her for him.

The Magician finally receives the kiss he has always wanted. They stand embraced in front of each other naked only hearing the rise and fall of each others breath. Raven then begins to think of the love she shared with Mr. White and grows concerned of his well being for she begins to reminisce the fateful day the Magician kissed her on top the clock tower and she fell to her immortality. "What have you done to Alistair White..? Mr. White. What have you done now?" she anxiously asks him. "I am sorry Raven, I sent the Fakir to assassinate White once I knew your presence would be occupied here. I cannot have you love him. I want your love only for myself," he says as he plunges his head into her neck. Raven's eyes fill with despair as she had fallen in love with Mr. White, a simple and pure love. "No, no no no!" she cries. She reaches for the dagger in his heart and pulls it out completely letting the blood pour out of his heart. He collapses to the floor and screams in agony, "How have you caused me so much pain Raven! Why do I hurt so badly? I'm not one to feel pain!" he yells at her rolling on the floor in his own bloodshed and agony as she runs to leave hurrying to dress and suit back on her weapons. The Magician lays on the floor fearfully reaching out for her. "Cassidy don't leave me. Please stay with me!" he cries out to her.

"You don't have time to save both Raven! You have to decide whom you love more dearly. Your best friend or your sweet lover. By the time the sun comes up both will perish and like I said you don't have a key to open that door!" Raven puts the copper dagger back in its holster and looks at his face of desperation. "I am sorry Samael but I have to end your rule of tyranny. She pulls out out of a tightly zipped pocket her two sacred keys. The holy keys shine brightly across the room piercing his eye. He gasps with disbelief, "It can't be! It can't be! There is no way you have those keys! How did you get them? How?!" He screams at her trying to crawl his way to her. Cassidy heads to his altar as something she spots grabs her attention. "What are you doing Cassidy? What are you doing over there?" he asks with wide concerning eyes. Cassidy rummages around to find the beautiful golden chain she spotted. She takes his chain and loops the two keys through the chain and braces it behind her neck securely. The Magician can not take his eyes off the keys. "That gold key... You hold the key!" he shouts in disbelief. Cassidy turns around to him with the two keys now hanging over her heart, "I think I can open that door." she says to him. The Magician's eyes fill with anger and jealousy, "There is no way you can save Mr. White. He is surely dead by now!" He shouts at her. Cassidy smirks out the side of her face, "Well we will see about that. I am pretty good at playing cards, especially solitaire," she replies. "I am always one step ahead in my own game."

The Magician looking perplexed at her radiating confidence begins to weep on the floor. Cassidy goes to him and uses a white sheet from the bed to drape over his naked body and she picks him up in her arms gracefully. All the Magician can do is weep in accepting his defeat. She holds him in her arms like a child and caries him through the halls and entering the chambers below. She carries him all the way to the very last vault. Arriving at the bottomless pit of the world the door opens at once in her presence for all unseen can see that she holds the key. As the door opens Cassidy hears the cry and moaning out of the dark of her dearly beloved friend and father figure. "Cassidy? Is that you?" he whispers. "Yes Slinger it is me. I am here to save you like I said I would," Cassidy replies with a tear filled smile.

Suddenly a vast array of light from no source illuminates up the bottomless pit and now Raven can see all the room holds in its glory. It is coated in the rarest of jewels and precious metals of sorts but no were to be seen is a place to rest nor food to eat and no water to drink. She gently places the Magician down upon a table of pure gold gently wrapped in his white cloth as he continues to weep of his destined fate. "I have to leave you here Samael for it is written. This key will lock you here and no one shall open it but me. I can not have you spread darkness and conquest like a disease infecting souls with your never ending search for more power," she says to him. "No Cassidy, remember it will always be a battle of light and dark. All must obey the light, but I am in no shame for who I am," replies the Magician. "I understand you are necessary Samael but that doesn't take away the responsibility of noble and righteous souls to stand for justice and peace. So here I stand obliging to what is fair and just," Cassidy replies.

"Was it really me that caused you pain Cassidy? Or was it that you were weak?" the Magician asks her. Raven stands back to pause in thought, "Yes I was weak. I betrayed myself, my soul, the greatest sin of all. Your ways can bring the brightest of souls to the darkest of places but I conquered and overcame you," she replies and leans forward to kiss his cupid shaped lips,

"A part of me does love you. I am sorry for what has to be," she says and comes up from her kiss. "Raven, one day you will see how needed I am in this world and you will set me free. I released you from your cage and someday you will release me from mine," he replies. Cassidy looks in through his eyes seeing a glimpse of innocence. "How did you release me?" she asks. "You always had the magic to set yourself free," he replies, "And that's how you will see someday why I am necessary my love."

CHAPTER 14

THE SUN

Cassidy goes to lift Slinger off the table and helps his weak body to stand. He embraces her dearly. "I though I would be here for eternity Cassidy. You are my hero," Slinger says to her. Cassidy and Slinger go to leave the room and before exiting she looks back one last time at the Magician. His heavy eyes gaze into hers from across the room, "I love you Raven and I will see you soon my child," he says to her. She exits the vault with a heavy heart and the door slams shut echoing throughout all the chambers of the underworld. Cassidy assists Slinger to walk up and out of the long halls of the chambers and journey up the stairs. "What about Mr. White? Do you think he is dead by now?" Slinger asks her very concerned as they finally exit the entry door to the chambers and head to the foyer in the mansion. "I am pretty sure a good friend had a change of heart and had a helping hand," Cassidy says smiling. She heads out the front doors of the mansion and the morning sun in the east is about to peak over the horizon giving a magnificent purple allure in the sky.

Loud thuds thunder through the earth and Cassidy quickly recognizes that as the sound of the giant making his way. Abatu comes over the horizon with a grin as wide as the sky holding Mr. White in his arms. She stands awaiting for him to make his way over to her with each giant step. He comes and kneels to her presence placing White on the ground in front of her as he rolls him out of his giant and now gentle hands. Cassidy ever so pleased looks up at Abatu. "My heart began to soften, just in time. Almost to late," Abatu says to her, "You saved me Raven. You saved me from myself."

The new sun begins to peak over the horizon permeating light throughout the world. Raven walks toward the sun and embraces this new day. "I will see you all soon," she says to the three men Abatu, Slinger, and White. Raven then runs to the sun and lifts herself high into the sky. She embarks to her home where the beginning and the end meet forever.

THE END

The Sun

The Sun

Made in the USA
Las Vegas, NV
22 January 2021